Howard's hands parte
descended towards th
eating me out. He tipp
licking at the drops which ran down his palms. I
kissed him, forcing my tongue between his lips and
sucking out as much of the unique blend as he
would allow me . . .

BRUNETTE

An erotic autobiography

Also available from Futura

Brunette

by

Anonymous

Futura

A Futura Book

First published in Great Britain in 1984
by Futura Publications, a Division of
Macdonald & Co (Publishers) Ltd
London & Sydney
Reprinted 1987, 1988, 1990 (twice)

ISBN 0 7088 2545 1

Printed and bound in Great Britain by
BPCC Hazell Books
Aylesbury, Bucks, England
Member of BPCC Ltd.

Futura Publications
A Division of
Macdonald & Co (Publishers) Ltd
Orbit House
1 New Fetter Lane
London EC4A 1AR

A member of Maxwell Macmillan Pergamon Publishing Corporation

Chapter One

It was a terrific car, I had to admit. Normally I wasn't that bothered about them. So long as my vehicle started properly and was simple to drive, that was all I wanted. I didn't really care about it looking flash or sleek, because those low slung sports cars are so difficult to climb in and out of for a girl. It's okay if you don't mind giving everyone in view an eyeful of cunt, but why should they see it for nothing?

And when you're low down, it's difficult to see the road ahead properly. I always felt vulnerable, as though a forty-ton truck could roll over such a car with me inside without even being aware of it. There are always so many controls and lights and dials and digital displays in modern cars. I've no idea what most of them are for, and I'm sure the majority of them aren't needed. The more complex things are, the more likely they are to go wrong.

I was once allowed by its proud owner to drive a 1930 vehicle, and that was great fun. There were just three pedals and two levers, which are still basic to most cars. I've never minded using gears, though I know a lot of women prefer automatics – or perhaps that's a male idea, they think women can't work out gears properly and so the idea of automatics has been foisted on us. With the old car, I had to double de-clutch, the handbrake didn't really work, the thing was heavy on the steering and shook and rattled a lot. There was only one dial, the speedometer. To find out how much petrol there was, you used a dipstick, just like checking the oil. There was a button on the floor to dip the headlights – and the whole light assembly actually moved. But when driving, I actually felt in contact with the road, because I could feel every bump, hear the engine and gearbox; and I knew how fast I was going by the way the wind whistled through the gaps in the canvas roof and blew my hair.

I'm sure such a car was much safer to drive. It would go just as fast as a modern car, or as fast as most cars do because of today's volume of traffic. But without a heater, a stereo cassette player, power steering, I really knew I was driving – not sitting at home in front of a television screen which showed a road and traffic. And of course there was far much less to go wrong. That was why the car was still around over half a century later, which won't happen to today's vehicles; they become obsolete and rusty within a year.

I was thinking of all this when I drove back to the garage half an hour after the service manager had told me that my car had been thoroughly checked and overhauled, and there was nothing wrong with it. It was brand new, I'd had it a week, a present from an admirer – the man who'd been fucking me the past month.

But there was still the same fault as before, a pulling back when my right foot was hard down and the rev counter almost hit the red zone.

The guy at the garage clearly didn't believe me, probably thought I was just a dumb woman who shouldn't have been driving such a fast and expensive car anyway. He tried to silence me with all kinds of technical jargon, but I wasn't having any of it.

'Come for a test ride in it,' I told him, 'that'll prove it.'

'I'm sorry,' he replied, 'but I don't have time.' He was lying; when I'd returned he'd been reading a newspaper.

'In that case,' I said, 'you can keep the car. I don't want it. You'll be hearing from my lawyers.' I threw the keys onto the desk in front of him and turned to go.

I wasn't bluffing. I liked the car, but it was no use if it wasn't perfect. If it was like this when new, what

6

would it be like in a year? I probably wouldn't keep it so long, but that wasn't the point. It was a matter of principle, and I wasn't going to let the garage get away with it.

'Just a minute, just a minute,' the man said hurriedly. 'I said I don't have time, but one of the mechanics could go with you. Would that be satisfactory?'

I turned and nodded my head, glancing at my watch to demonstrate that my time was equally as valuable.

'I won't be long.' The guy vanished through the door into the workshop.

I walked out to the forecourt and stood by the car. A minute later the man returned, and with him was a younger man. The mechanic was about twenty, tall with blond curly hair, dressed in a pair of greasy overalls.

'Go for a drive with this lady, Harry,' the service manager was saying, 'and see if you can identify the fault in the acceleration.'

Harry nodded, his eyes taking in the car before he looked at me.

'He's not getting in this car,' I said.

The mechanic frowned.

'Why not?' asked the older man.

'Not with those dirty clothes on,' I told them. 'The car will get filthy.'

Harry shrugged, unzipped his overalls and let them drop. He picked them up, rolling them into a ball which he threw back towards the entrance. He was wearing a pair of tight blue jeans and a short-sleeved white T-shirt, both of which emphasized his lithe muscular body.

I slid into the driving seat, and the mechanic climbed in through the passenger door. As I turned the key, the engine roared into life. I slammed the gear stick into first and accelerated away, the tyres screeching, and we thundered onto the road.

'I hope I'm not taking you away from anything important,' I said.

7

'That's okay,' Harry said. 'I'm glad of any excuse to stop working. What's the problem?'

I told him, and he nodded.

'Okay,' he said, 'just drive around and we'll see.' He leaned back on the sheepskin-covered seat, watching both the road ahead and the way I was driving – and me.

It was a warm day, and I drove with my window down, the slipstream blowing my long dark brown hair back over my shoulders. I was wearing loose and brief clothes: a pair of leather sandals, a short white cotton skirt and a red cheesecloth blouse, which was unbuttoned so low that my companion must have known I had no bra.

When we reached the open road, the car zoomed forward, faltered slightly, then resumed its acceleration. I glanced at the mechanic, and he nodded slightly.

'Slow down,' he said, looking back over his shoulder to check there was no traffic behind us, 'then come up through the gears as fast as you can.'

I did as he suggested, and the same thing happened again.

'Seems like the carbs,' he said. 'Pull over as soon as you can.'

Finding a side road, I slowed and turned. Harry climbed out.

'Open her up, please,' he asked. He took a look at the engine for a few seconds, then came back to my window. 'Have you got a pair of nail scissors?'

Automatically, I looked at his fingernails, which were black with grease. 'Giving yourself a manicure?' I asked, reaching behind for my bag and finding what he'd requested.

He grinned, shaking his head, then disappeared gain.

'That should do it,' he said, a minute later, handing back the scissors. 'Let's go for another ride.'

'Would you like to drive?' I suggested.

His eyes widened. 'Could I?' he asked eagerly, and he glanced at the car as if seeing it for the first time.

'Why not?' I slid across to the other seat. 'You're the expert. Climb aboard.'

Harry sat behind the wheel, staring at all the instruments. 'I've never driven one of these before, not on the open road.'

'Be my guest.'

He drove the car as though it had been his all his life, shifting expertly through the gears as the speedometer raced up the dial, and I realized that we'd gone through the problem spot without any trouble – or perhaps I hadn't noticed, because I'd been concentrating on the young man by my side, gazing at his rugged good looks and trying not to make it too obvious.

Harry slowed right down, then took the rev counter almost to maximum, the surge of acceleration pinning me back in my seat. He kept on driving, taking us further and further away from the garage, until he finally pulled in by the side of the road, the car skidding to a halt in a cloud of dust.

'Seems fine to me now,' he said. 'You want to try it for yourself?'

'No,' I said, 'I can tell you're right. That's great, really great. I must give you something for this.' I stretched across to the back seat to pick up my bag again.

But Harry shook his head. 'No, that's okay. It was a pleasure to drive your car. And as I said, I was glad to get away from work.'

'Fancy staying away a little longer?' I nodded towards a building a few hundred yards further down the road, a country inn. 'At least you could let me buy you a drink.'

Harry licked his lips. 'I ought to be getting back really.'

I said nothing, and he glanced at me.

'But I suppose it is almost lunch time,' he continued, nodding to himself, 'and it did take longer to locate the trouble than I expected . . .'

He glanced in the rearview mirror, and then the car was back on the road, like a jet fighter about to take off. No sooner had he reached top gear than he had to change down again, and in seconds we were stopped in the car park outside the inn. We went inside for the drinks, Harry ordering a bottle of beer while I had a vodka and lime, but we returned outside to sit at one of the tables. Because of the heat, the first drinks soon went down, and so we had another – then another.

'What time is it?' Harry asked. When I told him, he sighed. 'Better be getting back to work,' he muttered. But he made no move to leave the table.

'I know what you're thinking,' I said, watching his big green eyes as he looked at me. He was staring quite openly now, at my tanned thighs and the swell of my breasts.

'What's that?'

'About what a lovely day it is,' I told him, 'how nice it is to sit out here, doing nothing. How awful it is to have to go back to work when instead you could . . .' Casually, I stroked one of the empty beer bottles, making a circle of my thumb and forefinger and sliding it up and down the neck.

'Could what?' Harry prompted.

I shrugged. 'Whatever you like. Go for a ride in my car, perhaps. Would you like that? You can drive. Take me anywhere you want.'

'You don't have to do anything this afternoon, go anywhere?' he asked.

'I do what I please,' I said, picking the slice of lime from my empty glass and sucking out the bitter juice. 'And I'm going for a drive.' I stood up and began walking back to the car.

Harry hurried to catch up. 'What about me?' he asked. 'I can't stay here.'

'That's up to you.'

'We could have had a breakdown,' he said slowly, 'and that might keep me away for hours.'

'It might,' I agreed, and I threw him the car keys.

He caught them, and we walked on to the car. Harry took the driving seat. I said nothing, because what he did was up to him. He started the engine, and when we reached the road he didn't turn back towards the city. I rested my palm on his denim-clad thigh and closed my eyes; I made myself comfortable, secure in his driving skill, letting him take me where he would.

The car twisted and turned, accelerated and slowed, and finally it came to a halt. I opened my eyes. We were off the road, having turned up a dirt track and parked behind a row of trees. Harry switched off the engine.

My hand was still on his leg, and slowly I slid it up towards his crotch. The mechanic simply sat without moving, his hands still clutching the steering wheel. I felt the hardness of his young cock trying to thrust free from the confines of his tight jeans, and so I unzipped the denims to liberate it, smiling as I saw the fleshy rod spring out. It was slim and long, so pale and beautiful, its foreskin sliding back to reveal the darker hue of the swelling glans.

I watched it in admiration for several seconds, denying myself the satisfaction of touching it in order to increase my pleasure when I did. As soon as my fingertips caressed its stiff warmness, Harry came to life. He turned to face me, his hands reaching out for my shoulders and pulling me towards him.

We kissed. There was no subtlety about his technique, his tongue slipped immediately between my lips and probed for my own tongue. I responded with equal ferocity, and I felt one of his hands exploring beneath my skirt while the other cupped my nearest breast. His fingers tugged at the fabric of my brief panties, and I raised my buttocks, allowing him to yank the garment down my legs. Then his hand was on my pubic hairs, a single finger delving through for the heart of my cunt, which was already wet with lustful expectation. His other hand roughly undid my blouse, tearing the buttons off, and I felt his strong

11

fingers on my boobs, gently squeezing the hardness of my nipples.

I stroked at his cock, trying to unfasten his jeans but not succeeding. Suddenly both of Harry's hands left my flesh, and I fell backwards with a thump. He'd released my seat, which had tilted back until it was almost horizontal. He did the same to his own, but before he could dive on me again, I ensured that I'd pushed his pants down to his knees. I gazed at his prick; it was too long since I'd had a young man's knob inside me. His cock hairs were as blond as those on his head and even curlier.

I raised my skirt around my waist, allowing him to gaze at my twat for the first time, spreading my legs so he could see my moist labia and swollen clit. That was all the invitation that he needed.

He eased his way between my thighs, and climbed on top of me. The end of his cock slid over my cunt lips, causing me to tremble with delight, and a moment later he had taken proper aim and shoved the length of his tool deep within me. The sensation of his hardness rubbing against the walls of my vagina was wonderful, and it was even better when he began to fuck me.

My hands stroked his bare buttocks while his lips came down on my tits, sucking and lightly chewing each of my nipples in turn. His hips jerked back and forth as he thrust into me, and I rocked up and down to double the intensity of his stroke, already feeling the first flickering tremor of orgasm beginning to develop deep within me.

We fucked hard and urgently as though our lives depended upon it. To some extent this was true, because I couldn't live without fucking. We still wore our clothes, although my skirt was rolled up around my waist and my blouse completely unfastened; but Harry still had on his T-shirt, while his denims hung at his knees.

12

Our heartbeats were racing, our breath came rapidly, and beads of sweat covered our bodies.

Then the muscles of Harry's buttocks tautened, and I knew what that meant. He was about to come. I tensed the muscles of my cunt against his sliding shaft, trying to bring myself off before it was too late. My own climax was also imminent.

Suddenly I was flooded with hot pulsing semen, which squirted and splashed against the lining of my twat – and sparked off my own explosive orgasm. As Harry's hips thrust deep into me, I clasped him close and moaned in ecstasy, my fingernails digging deep into him. The man collapsed on top of me with a blissful sigh.

We lay without moving for a million years, and finally I began to stroke the mechanic's blond hair. He withdrew his cock, and stretched out on the seat next to me. His penis was smaller now and half limp, but it still looked so delicious. I unfastened my skirt and let my blouse fall off my shoulders as I rose to my knees, turning towards Harry's prick.

I took it in my hand, and it was all wet with both his come and mine. I kissed the tip, my tongue flicking out to sample the divine taste of our love juices. Harry's cock was irresistible, and my lips explored its length down to his testicles, then moved back to the purple glans. My mouth opened wide to engulf as much of the shaft as I could swallow.

Harry's hands were on my thighs, pulling at me, urging me to straddle his face. I knelt above him, and I felt his hot breath on my cunt, then the wetness as his tongue stroked my inner labia and gently sucked my clitoris.

Suddenly the phone rang, and we both froze.

'What the fuck . . . ?' said Harry.

I let his prick slip from between my lips, and I giggled. The telephone was in the glove compartment. William wanted it installed so that we could always

13

contact each other when we were on the road. I couldn't really object since it was him who'd paid for the car.

I fumbled for the receiver, picking it up and putting it to my lips. I was supporting myself on one elbow, holding the phone in my left hand, Harry's dick in the other.

'Hello,' I said.

'That you, baby?' asked William.

'Yes, William,' I answered.

'How's everything going?'

'Oh, fine, just fine.' I moved the mouthpiece back a little so there was room for the mechanic's cock; I gave it a swift lick. His oral affection had temporarily stopped, and so I wiggled my behind to encourage him to continue. He got the message, and I felt his tongue slide into my twat once more.

'Did you get the car fixed?' William wanted to know.

'Yes, it's been done.'

'Any problems?'

'No, none at all.'

'I told you that's a good garage. Any trouble and they'll sort it out for you.'

'Yes, you were right.'

'So,' he asked, 'what are you doing now?'

I kissed the tip of Harry's knob; it was beginning to grow again. 'Oh, nothing much,' I said, 'just driving around.'

'But you're enjoying yourself?'

'Yes,' I said, my eyes closing in sheer delight as Harry at last targeted his tongue on my clitoris. As a reward, I circled my lips around the ridge behind his glans, my tongue caressing its domed end.

'That's what I like to hear.'

I panted for breath. 'What about you?' I asked. 'Will you be back tonight?' Because if he wasn't, I had plans – plans which involved the guy currently so busy eating my cunt.

William said he wouldn't be, that he had more business to attend to during the afternoon. Then he

14

told me where he was, and I had to suppress a laugh. He was in my home town, the place where I'd spent most of my life but had hardly even thought of recently.

But as William chattered inanely on, I didn't listen. I was too busy enjoying the way the blond mechanic licked my twat so divinely, and while I sucked silently on Harry's firm cock, I was remembering how much had happened to me over the past few years.

Chapter Two

My best friend was a boy called Mark. We'd been friends ever since I could remember, because we'd always lived next door to each other. He was a year older than me, but we still went to the same school. Mark used to take a lot of ribbing from the other boys for spending so much time with me, particularly when he was younger; but between us we could take on and beat any other two boys in school.

I never thought much of other girls; they were so soppy, always playing with dolls and helping their mothers clean up the house. I much preferred climbing trees and playing football. Once I'd proved myself, I would usually be accepted into one of the local gangs of boys which were constantly splitting and reforming. I could have been taken for a boy, because of my slim figure and short dark brown hair; and I always wore jeans, because I hated dresses and skirts.

There were often initiation ceremonies which had to be gone through, most of which seemed to involve the boys showing off their penises to one another. Even before they were teenagers, they were already obsessed with the size of their cocks. By the time I was ten, I'd probably seen more dicks than most women ever do. But there was a difference, of course – a difference I was only to discover a few years later.

Naturally I couldn't pass any of their ritual exhibitions which involved discovering who could piss the furthest or highest against a wall, although I did try out my own variations which involved standing on my hands and bracing my feet against the target wall . . .

The boys had cocks, but I didn't. I wished I'd been a boy, but I didn't wish that I had a knob of my own.

There's some highbrow theory about girls who have penis envy, although I'm convinced I never felt that way. If I did, I've certainly had enough pricks since to more than make up for it!

But at that sort of age, none of us were bothered about the different biological equipment which had been assigned to each sex. Kids first become curious about that kind of thing when they are three to four years old, then they lose interest for about a decade until they carry on where they left off.

And that's exactly what happened to me.

I can't remember precisely how old I was when my interest was rekindled, but I can never forget the incident which provoked my sexual awakening.

As I said, Mark and I were best friends; but even when the others in our classes were beginning to take an interest in the opposite sex, our relationship was the same as it always had been – we'd hate each other one day, spend all our time together the next. There was no way that I was his 'girlfriend' or he my 'boyfriend', it was completely platonic. We'd go to the movies together, or roller skating, but that was because we each found the other such good company. We had the same interests in records and comics, we supported the same football team – and Mark could help me with my homework, because he'd been through exactly the same lessons the previous year.

We'd always been about the same size, but over the past year Mark had suddenly shot up so that he was six inches taller than me. I'd also begun to grow, although in a different direction. Much to my annoyance, my breasts began to develop. I hated them, because they upset my balance when I ran, and they bounced up and down and looked so stupid.

The key event happened one Saturday afternoon when I went around to Mark's house. I'd been there in the morning, and we'd been up in his room playing records. There was a new album I'd bought with my pocket money on the way home from school the evening before, and I discovered that I'd left it at Mark's. So I went back to collect it.

My parents were in the front room of our house, and I climbed over the fence to get into the back of Mark's place. They didn't like me doing that, because it wasn't 'ladylike'. But who the hell wanted to be a lady? I also had to make sure that my little brother wasn't watching. John was at that horrible sneaky age where he delighted in telling tales about me.

Mark's parents were out, I'd heard their car drive away before, which meant they wouldn't notice me climbing over the fence either. Mark was lucky, he didn't have any brothers or sisters who could act as informers.

I went up to the back door and pulled it open, entering Mark's house via the kitchen. Silently, I crept through into the front room, where I expected him to be. The television was on, and I guessed he'd have been watching the sports programme. He wasn't there and must have been upstairs, so I took a seat and waited for him to come down. After five minutes he still hadn't appeared.

I could have shouted for him, but instead I decided to surprise him. And I certainly did . . .

Without a sound, I made my way up the stairs. I thought Mark might have been in the bathroom, and I could have jumped out at him and given him a scare when he emerged. But the door was open, so he couldn't have been. All the other upstairs doors were open except one, and that was his bedroom.

Putting my ear to the door, I listened; but I could hear nothing. Perhaps he wasn't in there, wasn't in the house at all. He must have gone out with his parents. In that case, I might as well go inside and collect my record.

I took hold of the door handle, turned it, pushed the door open, took a step inside – and then I froze, staring.

Staring at Mark, who was in there. Lying on his bed.

Naked. Holding his dick in one hand. And it was enormous, much bigger than it had been the last time I'd seen it, a few years ago. It was thick and hard, pointing upwards instead of hanging down, and his clenched hand was frantically stroking the thing. His face was contorted, his mouth wide open, and he panted for air. He looked in pain.

His eyes were closed, so he didn't notice me at first.

I couldn't move, I gazed in dumb amazement at Mark. What was he doing?

Then I noticed that there was a magazine lying on the bed next to him. It was the kind of thing I'd sometimes come across in the shed at the end of our garden, hidden behind the old flowerpots or rusty shears. My father used to put them there. I didn't know why. They were full of photographs of naked women. And I could see Mark's magazine was the same, wide open in the centre pages to show a nude girl.

As I stared, Mark's hand became still and his eyes opened. He saw me and he gasped. At the same moment, his firm cock began to twitch and suddenly shot a jet of liquid onto his chest. My first thought was that he was peeing, but it wasn't like that. The stuff squirted out in brief pulses, and it was white and creamy.

Mark tried to cover his groin with both hands, but the tip of his cock gushed out another foaming spurt, which oozed through his fingers and dripped thickly onto his stomach.

We were both still staring at one another, and I didn't know which one of us was the more embarrassed. Neither of us moved for several seconds, and then I swiftly spun around, fled from the room, dashed down the stairs, twisted around the hall, sprinted into the kitchen, burst through the back door leapt over the fence and was back in my house and heading for the safety of my own room in a matter of seconds

I didn't see Mark again that day and as I lay awake in bed at night I thought of what 'd seen, rev· · σ the memory over and over, finding it oddly exciting. I became aware of my nipples standing out and pressing against the fabric of my pyjamas, and I wasn't even cold. Sliding my hands onto my chest, I felt the hardness of my pink nipples, stroking them with my palm and enjoying the sensation.

Leaving my left hand on my right breast, my other hand slipped down inside my waistband and onto the place between my legs where I'd have had a cock if I'd been a boy, touching the soft silkiness of my newly grown hairs. Mark had been hairy there, too, I remembered.

But why had his cock been like that? Was that what happened to boys around the same age that their voices broke? Their dicks began to point upwards, just like girls grew boobs? The question I most wanted answering, however, was: What on earth had Mark been doing . . . ?

We'd never had sex education lessons at school, and although my mother had told me briefly about puberty, I was almost totally ignorant. I'd heard the other girls in my class laughing and giggling, whispering to one another about their boyfriends; but as I didn't have much contact with these girls, I wasn't able to pick up any information from them. I hadn't been that interested, either – not until now.

I didn't see Mark the following day. It was up to him to make the first move. If he wished to see me, he could come around. I wanted my new record, but I didn't dare to go and ask for it. Our bedrooms faced each other, separated only by the two garages built between our respective homes. I kept looking out of the window, ready to say something – although I wasn't sure what – if I saw Mark, but he must have been too ashamed to even look out.

What I did do that afternoon was make my way to the shed to see if there were any of those magazines still hidden there, the kind I'd seen Mark with. Perhaps that would give me a clue to what he'd been doing. I found a couple of them rolled up behind the lawn mower. When I'd discovered some before, I merely glanced through them and looked at the cartoons. But few of them had made any sense, and none of them had been funny. I certainly hadn't bothered studying the colour pictures of the naked girls.

Now that was what I did, examining the glossy nudes which filled the majority of the pages. The girls were mostly naked, or wearing very little – just things like high-heeled shoes, maybe even black stockings. They'd be lying on a bed, or spread out in a chair or supine on the floor. And all the poses were so ridiculous, the way hardly any girl would sit or lie. I soon figured out the reason for this, it was so that they showed off one part of their anatomy more prominently.

I'd have suspected that they'd have been displaying the most obvious difference between men and women – or the difference which to me was so obvious, which showed up even under clothes: the fact that girls had tits, and men didn't.

But instead the emphasis was lower down. All the girls had their legs wide open, the photographic angle either from the front or the rear focusing on their vaginal lips. It surprised me how prominent they were, with swollen pink folds that I didn't know existed, but that was all. I found it very boring flicking through dozens of pictures of shiny-skinned women touching their boobs or else with their fingers against their crotches, and I couldn't understand what the attraction was.

Maybe Mark had been reading the magazine, because he couldn't possibly be interested in so many pictures of girls which were almost all identical. I started with the readers' letters, because mostly they were short and I hated having to read anything too long.

The first letters were all about a previous issue, tne guys saying how much they'd like the various girls, making comments about their figures and what they'd like to do to the models if they had the chance. I wasn't too sure about some of this, because there were unfamiliar words like 'cunt' and 'fuck' – I'd heard these at school, but they were only swear words; I didn't know that they meant anything. I managed to guess what 'cunt' meant, but then I became baffled again because 'twat' seemed to mean the same thing.

Then I found something which seemed applicable, it was from a man who talked about 'shooting his load' all over the centre pages of the magazine, and from his graphic description of rubbing his prick it seemed that this was exactly what I'd witnessed. I read on, trying to discover exactly why he'd done this and what it meant, but I wasn't able to get much further because I heard the back door of the house open, so I swiftly replaced the magazines and left the shed.

Mark and I always went to school together in the mornings. Whoever was ready first would go next door and call for the other one. But that Monday morning, even when I was ready, I sat at the bottom of the stairs because I didn't want to have to knock on Mark's door. I glanced at my watch, knowing I'd be late if I didn't leave in a minute or two.

Perhaps Mark was doing the same, just waiting for me to make the first move. The only solution was to pretend that everything was as usual, nothing had happened. I opened the door and went out, and as I reached the front gate I noticed that Mark was just coming out of his door. He hesitated as he saw me, and for a moment I thought that he was going back inside again. I waited for him, and he walked up to where I was standing.

'Hello,' I said.

'Hello,' he echoed, not meeting my eye.

We walked on side by side in silence. I wanted to say something, anything. I thought that I ought to apologize, but I didn't want to bring the subject up because I could tell he wouldn't like it. I'd gone into

22

his bedroom hundreds of times when he'd been in there, and he'd also come into my room so often without warning. It was only for Mark's sake that I didn't mention what had happened. For myself, I was bursting with curiosity – although my instincts told me it wouldn't be tactful to ask.

We said nothing until we reached the school gates. Usually we made our own way home in the evening, so this might be my last chance to talk to Mark all day. Therefore I spoke up at last.

'I left that new record of mine in your room on Saturday morning,' I said.

Mark nodded.

'Can I come around and pick it up?' I asked.

He nodded again.

'When?' I wanted to know.

This time he shrugged.

We'd come to a halt inside the entrance, because we both went in different directions from here. I wasn't going to let Mark escape without saying something, if only a word.

'When?' I repeated, and I moved around to block his route, making it clear that I wouldn't shift out of the way until he'd replied.

'Whenever you want,' he said at last.

'You're sure?' I asked.

'Sure I'm sure,' he said impatiently. 'I've told you, haven't I?'

'Then I can come around any time?'

'Yeah,' said Mark.

He still hadn't looked at me directly, but now I moved out of the way so that he could pass. He walked by me, and I turned around to go my own way.

'Hey!' I heard him call.

I glanced around.

'Maybe you'd better knock next time,' he said, and slowly he smiled. Then he spun around and headed off towards his classroom.

I went around that very evening, and we played my record over Mark's stereo in his room. He'd got a much better system than mine, which is why I preferred to listen to music at his house.

We usually sat together on the bed, because that was the best position to pick up the proper stereo effect from the two speakers mounted in the opposite corners. No mention was made of the last time I'd arrived uninvited in his room, although Mark must have been thinking about it as much as I was.

I was remembering the magazine he'd had, which couldn't have been much different from the ones I'd studied in the shed the previous day. I was comparing myself to the nude girls, thinking of my own ripening breasts . . . and my cunt. And I became aware of the way Mark was watching me, studying me from the corner of his eyes as though he'd never seen me before. I'd noticed this recently, but I hadn't paid much attention – just as I hadn't really bothered about the way he sometimes seemed to touch me more than accidentally . . . such as how his hand would rest on my thigh as he spoke to me, or the way his arm brushed against my breasts as he leaned down to reach for a book.

I found myself gazing at his crotch, at the folds in his denims, thinking that they seemed far too tight to contain the rod of flesh I'd seen a couple of days earlier, but aware of an unmistakable bulge.

Finally it was time to go, and I replaced my record in its sleeve and stood up. We usually only spent one evening a week together, either at my house or Mark's or maybe at the movies, because the rest of the time was taken up with homework. Mark intended to go to university, or rather that was his parents' plan; and so they didn't like him spending too much time with me when he should have been studying. Revising for exams was all a myth where Mark was concerned, because school work came so easy to him. He was very clever, but he never spoke down to me, which is one

24

of the reasons why I liked him so much. I hated school and couldn't wait to leave.

'See you tomorrow morning,' said Mark, as he also rose to his feet. He glanced at his bedroom door. It was half open. His parents didn't like him and me to be alone in his room with the door shut, and I still wasn't aware of the reason why . . .

'Yeah,' I agreed, but I didn't move. I could tell that Mark wanted to say something else, and I waited for what it might be, staring up at him into his big green eyes, aware of what a good looking boy Mark was. Tall and lean, slim-hipped, his hair a tangled mass of jet black curls. For a moment I thought of his other black curls I'd seen and the length of flesh which had seemed to grow from them.

Mark licked at his dry lips, and unconsciously I imitated his gesture.

And suddenly, as if telepathically, I realized that Mark wanted to kiss me. A few days ago the idea would have repulsed me, but as I gazed at his soft lips I could feel myself trembling inside – and right at that moment I wanted him to take me in his arms, crush me against him, his mouth fiercely coming down against mine, and I'd be his slave, unable to resist. I felt like the heroine in one of those dumb romantic comics the other girls had, but I couldn't help it.

'Don't be late,' said Mark.

And the moment was gone.

'Okay,' I agreed, both disappointed and relieved.

We walked downstairs, Mark opened the front door, and I went home. I fixed a cheese sandwich for supper and made a pot of tea for myself and my parents. John was already in bed by then. I poured the tea, then carried it into the front room on a tray, and I watched television while I ate. Then I said goodnight and climbed the stairs to bed. After having a quick wash and cleaning my teeth, I went into my bedroom.

I glanced out of the window towards Mark's room, but I could see nothing through the darkness; he didn't have his light on. I kicked off my sneakers, then pulled off my T-shirt and jeans, throwing them onto the chair next to the bed. There was a full-length mirror on the wardrobe door, and I stared at my reflection. I still wore my hair very short, because it was far less bother to wash and comb than when it was longer; but I wondered what it would look like if I grew it out, thinking that perhaps I'd give it a try.

As I studied myself, I thought again of those magazine pictures of the nude girls. I was wearing a pair of red stretchy panties and a white bra, and I peeled them off. It was only recently that I'd bought the bra, having resigned myself to the fact that I was stuck with my tits.

I stared at my naked body, turning in profile to study my boobs, then gazing at my crotch with its nest of hairs. At first, when I'd noticed the new hairs growing, I'd been worried; they weren't like the fine downy ones on my arms and legs. I'd thought I was turning into a werewolf or something, but by now I was used to them and I liked the contrast of colour against my pale flesh.

I ran my fingers through the hairs, remembering the emphasis in all of the glossy photographs, and I spread my legs a little, my right index finger tracing the line of the vertical cleft which ran downwards and between my legs. Then I grinned at myself, turning away towards the bed and searching for my pyjamas amongst the rumpled covers, finding and putting them on.

Feeling tired, I didn't bother with the lamp once I'd switched off the main light; it was too late to read. I climbed into bed, tugging the blankets up all around me as I snuggled down and closed my eyes.

After a while, I became aware of a dim light flickering on and off. If it had stayed constant, I would hardly have noticed. But the illumination came on for a few seconds, followed by darkness, and I'd think that it had gone away, but then suddenly it would return. I opened my eyes, watching the pattern of light which came through the window and spread across my pillow and bedspread.

I sat up in bed, looking out, and I saw that the source of rhythmic brightness was Mark's bedroom, which like mine was the only window on that side of the house. He kept switching his light on and off. We hadn't used such semaphore to signal one another for years. Around the same time we'd rigged up a pulley between our rooms, so that we could send messages to one another or swap comics.

Even after so long, I still knew the routine. I couldn't see Mark, but I signalled him by flicking my lamp on and off, on and off. And the next time his light went on, it stayed on, and I was able to see right into his room as he walked towards the window, looking across to me.

I stared in astonishment, because he was naked again, and I could clearly see his upright penis, the top stretching almost as high as his navel. He wasn't holding it, not this time, his cock was standing up without any help.

Mark stood in front of the window, looking towards me. Although my room was dark and Mark couldn't see me, it was obvious he had wanted me to look at him and guessed that I was. That was why he'd signalled me with the light.

I watched fascinated, although I couldn't see properly because the front of his body was now in shadow, but I was aware that his hard knob was pressed up against the glass. I wondered if he was going to start manipulating it up and down, but instead he suddenly drew the curtains and was gone.

For a couple of minutes I didn't move, thinking that perhaps Mark would open the curtains again for an encore. But then the light went off, and so I lay down once more.

I stayed awake for a long time, my mind and body a turmoil of feelings and emotions which I'd never felt before and couldn't explain.

Chapter Three

Although we went to school together every morning for the rest of the week, neither of us mentioned the incident. I kept watching Mark's window the next five nights, but there was no repeat performance. Nor did I find the opportunity to visit the garden shed again to improve my education.

On Saturday afternoon, exactly a week after I'd seen Mark 'shooting his load', I was sitting in my bedroom playing a cassette I'd borrowed from him when I heard what sounded like a knock on my window, which was almost what it was. Rising to my feet, I went to look out. I saw Mark leaning out of his window; he'd thrown a pebble to attract my attention. I opened the window.

'Hi,' said Mark.

'Hi yourself,' I said, wondering what he wanted.

'Doing anything?' he asked.

I shrugged. 'Not much.'

'Why don't you come over?'

'Why not?' I agreed. 'Okay. Be there in a minute.'

I closed the window and switched off the cassette player before going downstairs. My mother was in the kitchen, so I couldn't take the short cut over the back fence. I went out of the front and around to Mark's house, noticing that the car wasn't in the drive. His parents were out.

There was no sign of Mark downstairs, so I presumed that he was still up in his room. I found him sitting on his bed, flicking through the pages of another girlie magazine; but at least he was dressed this time. He hardly glanced up at me as I entered. His stereo was on, but I hesitated before taking my normal place by his side. After a second I climbed onto the bed, sliding up to lean against the wall, looking over Mark's shoulder at the glossy pages.

'Ever seen one of these before?' he asked, tapping the magazine which was spread across him, turning to observe my reaction.

'Yes,' I said.

That seemed to throw him a moment, because all he said was a surprised 'oh'.

'I was thinking of growing my hair like hers,' I added, pointing to the model. Her hair was the same colour as mine, but Mark probably hadn't noticed her hair – or at least that on her head. She was wearing a translucent white blouse and a pair of lace-up sandals, but nothing in between, sitting on a beach with her knees drawn up towards her chin, legs apart so that her genitals could be clearly seen.

But Mark wasn't listening, and he repeated what he'd said before. 'Ever seen one of these before?'

I realized I'd been wrong, he wasn't dressed, not properly. Because as he pulled the magazine aside I could see that the top of his jeans was unfastened, the zip pulled all the way down – and poking out was his stiff cock.

'Yes,' I said, trying to sound equally as casual as I gazed down at his swollen tool.

Mark was still watching my face, studying my expression. I waited for him to say something, but eventually it was me who broke the silence.

'I've seen yours before lots of times,' I continued, hurriedly, at last looking away and meeting his eyes. 'In the old days, you know, and those of all the other boys who used to be in the gangs.'

'Doesn't it look different now?' Mark asked.

'No,' I said, shaking my head.

'You're not looking, go on, take a proper look.'

I did as I was told, staring at the rod of flesh which thrust up like some weird pink snake climbing out of its nest of black hairs.

'Well?' he prompted.

'It looks the same,' I said quietly. 'The same as it did when I saw it on Monday, and last Saturday when you were playing with it.' This was my chance. 'What were you doing, anyway?'

'I was doing what you said, playing with it. Like this.' So saying, he took his cock in his right hand and slid his fist up and down its length.

'Why?' I asked.

'Because it's nice. Don't you ever touch yourself down there?'

'No!' I said quickly.

'Really?' said Mark, as though he doubted me. 'You ought to, you'd like it. Or I think you'd like it. Boys like it, so girls must do as well.'

'I think I'd better be going,' I said. But I didn't move, I sat where I was, both repulsed and attracted by what Mark was doing.

'Do you know why it goes like this,' Mark asked, 'all big and hard?' I didn't reply, and he took my silence as a negative so he answered. 'It gets full of blood which makes it all stiff and ready for fucking.'

His hand was still lazily stroking himself, his eyes on my face, then on my breasts.

'You know what fucking is?' he wanted to know.

I shook my head slowly. My pulse had increased, and I suddenly felt very hot, tiny drops of sweat forming all over my body.

'It's when a man sticks his cock in a woman's cunt,' said Mark. 'That's what it is. He pushes it in and out, in and out, in and out.' As he spoke, his hand slid up and down, up and down, up and down his shaft. 'Then he comes, shoots his spunk into her cunt.' He licked his lips. 'That's what fucking is.'

I nodded. I wasn't really listening. It was as if Mark's voice was a long way off, not at all connected with what he was doing. And I kept watching, taking in every detail of his prick, from the dimpled hairiness of his balls to the small slit in the top which oozed a drop of shiny liquid.

'But . . . ?' I managed to say.

'You ought to read some of these,' Mark told me, nodding to the magazine by his side. 'They tell you all about sex. You'll never find that out in the sort of magazine girls have. That's all fashion and pop music. Do they tell you how to masturbate? Of course they don't.'

'Masturbate?' I asked. The word sounded familiar from the letter page in the magazine I'd seen last week.

'It's having sex with yourself,' said Mark. 'See? My hand's like a cunt, gripping my cock nice and tight. I close my eyes and imagine it's sliding into a juicy twat. Girls can do it, too.'

He must have noticed my disbelieving expression, because he said, 'They do. Girls can pretend that their own fingers are a cock, and they can slip them inside their cunts.'

'But . . .' I shook my head in bewilderment; I couldn't understand what he was saying. '. . . why?'

He grinned. 'Because it's so nice. Here, do you want to touch it?' He let go of his tool, reaching to grab my hand and pulling it towards his hard length of flesh.

I tore my fingers loose. 'No!' I said hurriedly. 'It's dirty!'

'It isn't,' Mark assured me, and he grinned slyly. 'Do you know that some girls even put penises in their mouths and lick and suck them?'

'Mark!'

'I'm serious, they really do.' He glanced down at his knob, then took hold of it again. 'You don't mind me doing this?'

'It's up to you,' I told him, trying to be nonchalant.

'It isn't dirty, you know. Sex isn't dirty, not at all. It's great, it really is.'

'How do you know?' I asked. 'You've never tried it have you?'

'Tried what?'

I hesitated. 'Sex.'

31

'Use the other word,' said Mark. 'Go on, you know the one.'

'Fucking,' I said defiantly. 'Fucking, fucking, fucking! You've never tried it, so how do you know it's so good?'

'If it's any better than jerking off, it must be fantastic.'

I shrugged. I was still thinking about what Mark had said a few seconds before – that some girls would let a boy put his cock in their mouth. I shuddered at the thought. I tried imagining one forcing its way into my cunt, and I didn't know which was worse. The idea of the first made me want to vomit, while the latter made my stomach all queasy.

Yet at the same time I had the urge to do as Mark had asked, to hold his cock in my hand. I was curious to know what it felt like.

Without realizing, my hand went to my own crotch, lightly brushing against my denims. I might not have been aware of it, but Mark had noticed.

'Why don't you pull your jeans down?' he suggested. 'Then you can finger-fuck yourself.'

'I wouldn't!'

'Yes, you would,' Mark told me, as his hand continued slowly pumping at his dick, gripping it in a circle made from thumb and forefinger, the flesh rippling up and down the shaft. 'I've seen you.'

I stared at him. 'You've what!'

He nodded towards the window, smiling slyly.

I gasped and climbed off the bed, staring out of the window across into my own room, it was hard to see in now but I could imagine what a good view Mark would have at night when the light was on, realizing how I never closed the curtains and remembering how over the last year or so I had begun touching myself – exploring my developing curves and feeling at my new pubic hairs.

At one time it wouldn't have bothered me that

anyone had seen me in the nude, let alone Mark; but now I was furious. I felt betrayed and cheated.

'I just love watching you take your clothes off,' said Mark. 'You've got a lovely body.' As he spoke, he began tugging at his jeans, pulling them off. 'Why don't you get undressed now?' He kicked off his denims then began unbuttoning his shirt. 'I love jerking off when you're in the nude. Why don't you strip off for me now, huh?' He threw his shirt aside and was naked. Both hands went to his groin, his left stroking his balls, his right clutching the shaft and beginning to manipulate it once more.

I backed away towards the door, shaking my head. This was terrible, awful, disgusting. I had to get away, to escape, and I rushed out of the door and speedily retreated to my own house, taking the stairs two at a time and slamming my bedroom door behind me. I leaned against the door, but even then I wasn't safe and I went down on all fours, creeping towards the window, reaching up for the curtains and pulling them shut.

Only then could I relax, and I sighed as I started ripping off my clothes. I felt all hot and sticky, I just had to have a shower. In a matter of seconds I was naked, and I caught sight of myself in the mirror and I smiled at my nude image, then shook my head as I thought about Mark. Why had I run away like that? I had nothing to fear from him. Okay, so he liked looking at me without my clothes. But so what? I liked it, too . . .

I supposed I'd been worried that he was going to touch me, but there was no way he could reach me now. As I stared into the mirror, I saw a mischievous smile form on my lips, and I turned away and walked towards the curtains, boldly drawing them back to stand naked in the window. The window ledge was very low, only as high as my knees, and so Mark would have had a perfect view of me. Better than ever, because I'd never stood nude up against the glass before.

The only trouble was that there was no sign of him.

I had a few pebbles in a bowl on the sill which I used to signal Mark, and so I unfastened the window and swung it wide open, hurling one of the small stones across the twenty foot gap between our two rooms. After so many years' practice, my aim was true and the pebble clattered against the glass and then bounced down onto the garage roof below.

A couple of seconds later, Mark's head appeared from the side of his window. When he saw the way I was dressed, or wasn't dressed, he also stepped out into the open. He was as naked as I, the angle of his prick still blatantly vertical.

I closed my window as we faced each other. Spreading my legs until my feet were as wide apart as I could stretch them, I leaned forward, raising my arms to grasp the curtains above and to either side of me, thrusting my crotch to and fro. It was the best view I could offer, and I watched as Mark took hold of his erect cock and continued masturbating.

His hand slid up and down, up and down, faster and faster, his mouth open wide as he gasped. Having told me that jerking off was enjoyable, I was able to interpret his expression as such; the division between pleasure and pain is a very fine line.

As I watched I could feel a strange stirring in my own crotch. The only way I could identify it was by comparing it to an itch. And the one way to get rid of an itch was to scratch it, but such a response wouldn't have been at all appropriate. The feeling was far too deep, it wouldn't be defeated so easily – and anyway I liked the sensation, not wanting it to go away. I didn't move, apart from continuing to rock my hips back and forth, my crotch pressing against the cold window pane and then retreating.

And then Mark came, his cock jetting its first spurt of whiteness high against his window. Then it pulsed and fountained again, and again, and again. Before I knew it, he had retreated out of sight, and all that was left were the glistening streaks of spunk which slowly trickled down the glass.

That night I tried what Mark had been talking about earlier. I stripped off, not caring if he might have been watching and not even interested, because it wasn't him I was interested in this time. It was myself.

I climbed naked between the sheets, closing my eyes, and I ran my fingers over my body. I tried to pretend that it was Mark touching me, not that I wanted Mark but he was the only person I could think of, and it was easy to imagine that they were his fingers which stroked my nipples, teasing them to firmness, then caressed my ribcage, the flesh of my stomach, sliding down to touch my hips and then further to lightly rub my thighs, all the time circling and spiralling towards the centre of my being, the triangle of dark hairs which marked the entrance to my femininity, tentatively brushing across it, pressing slightly harder and harder with my fingertips, my legs opening a fraction to admit the probe, finding the unknown contours which were already moist in anticipation of this exploration, sliding through the folds into the secret depths, gently stroking and rubbing . . .

It was pleasant, a warm glow suffusing my whole body; but it was no more than that – just pleasant. I wondered if I was doing something wrong, or maybe Mark had been exaggerating. Perhaps it was different for a girl. It had to be, because I didn't have a cock and there was no way that I could erupt as spectacularly as he had.

But it made me feel relaxed and contented, and I slept really well that night. The next day I decided that maybe the time wasn't right, I just hadn't matured enough so that my body could respond fully to my attempts at masturbation.

After that, however, Mark and I had regular sex sessions every week – or at least it was sex for him, although I wasn't totally disinterested in the process. He enjoyed jerking himself off more while I was there, and it didn't bother me, so why should I have denied him his fun? It was a lot less boring than homework.

The next time I went around there, Mark taught me more about what he was doing – increasing my vocabulary to include words like erection, orgasm and many more – while he lay stretched out on his bed, naked of course, stroking himself.

'You haven't got one of those magazines this time,' I pointed out.

'I don't need it,' he said, half smiling. 'Not when I've got you.'

'I'm not going to take my clothes off,' I emphasized.

Mark shrugged. 'That's okay. I've got a good memory.' His fist clutched his cock, sliding up and down.

I was sitting only a couple of feet away from him, on the edge of the bed, and I remembered the naked magazine girls, flattered that Mark claimed he was thinking of me rather than them. I felt at ease at last. The first time, when I'd surprised him, my main reaction had been astonishment; and last week I'd been tense when he'd suddenly begun jerking himself off.

But now there was no pressure at all, because I knew exactly what was going on – and I was curious to have a good look at the process. It had been very casual and informal. The night before Mark had said: 'Do you want to come around tomorrow while I masturbate?' And I'd replied: 'Okay.'

He'd taken his time stripping off, and first we'd talked about a television film we'd both seen the previous evening. I wasn't sure why Mark asked my opinion of it, because I knew he wasn't that interested in the programme. Only later did I realize that he'd been trying to concentrate on something boring and mundane in order to fool his eager cock, to make it wilt – so that when he dropped his pants I'd be able to watch it swell and grow. Which is what happened.

In the non-functional position, Mark's dick looked far more like the familiar flesh I'd seen so many times when we were younger. Its dimensions were much greater than they'd ever been in the old days, of course, and his testicles were no longer a small tight cluster but hung loosely between his legs.

Almost as soon as Mark removed his jeans, his cock began to expand, rising up like a flower lifting its head to the light. I stared in fascination at the speed. I'd never seen anything like it, a creature doubling its size in a matter of seconds, waking up, stirring, then rising high and straight, ready for action. Even when it was almost vertical, there was still movement, because the end of his cock kept on swelling, forcing itself free of the foreskin.

I knew it was the foreskin because Mark told me.

'Do you want to hold it?' he asked, nodding towards his prick.

I shook my head very decisively.

Mark sighed. 'No harm in asking,' he muttered. 'I don't suppose you want to take your clothes off, either?'

This was before he'd said that it was me he was thinking of while he stroked himself, but I shook my head again.

'Ah well,' he shrugged. 'Let's get going.' And that was when he'd started masturbating.

I sat watching, and he grinned at me while we kept talking.

'It's better to do it slowly,' he explained after a while, 'because then it feels even greater when it happens. I try not to do it too often, because there isn't as much spunk if I wank too much – and that's what it's all about. The more spunk, the more squirts I can get.' He removed his hand for a moment, spitting into his palm, then rubbing his saliva behind the ridge of his glans. That was another word he taught me.

'What's that for?' I asked.

'Lubrication, so it slides better. Works the same as cunt juice, I suppose. What's cunt juice like?'

I shrugged, unsure what to say – whether to reply that I didn't know and thus betray my ignorance – so I said nothing.

'Well,' said Mark, and he grinned wickedly, 'this is what cock juice is like!'

I glanced down, noticing that his hand had stopped moving, but that the end of his penis was aimed directly at me! Instinctively I jumped away just as Mark's cock began to spurt, and the first creamy streak shot onto the corner of the bed just where my thigh had been . . .

Seeing that he'd missed, he released his grip and his prick sprung back, the second and subsequent throws shooting onto his own stomach. Finally his cock stopped erupting and became still.

I stood at the foot of the bed, glaring at Mark. I was so mad I couldn't think of anything to say, but he simply grinned at me.

'I warned you to take your clothes off, didn't I?' he laughed. 'Anyway, it didn't hit you.'

'No thanks to you!' I said furiously. 'If you ever try that again, I'll . . . I'll . . .'

I took a couple of steps towards Mark, and I stretched out my hand, then flicked my right index finger hard against his wilting knob.

He howled, more in surprise than pain, and I realized that for the first time I'd touched his penis – although contact had lasted but an instant.

He glanced at me apologetically. 'Sorry. No harm done. It was just a joke.'

'I'm not laughing, Mark.'

'Okay, okay, I've said I'm sorry,' he told me. 'It would have been no great disaster. Spunk washes out. It doesn't stain, it doesn't smell of anything . . . and it doesn't taste of anything, either.'

'Doesn't taste?' I asked, wondering how he knew. Surely he couldn't have tried it . . . ?

'That's right,' said Mark, levering himself up on both elbows and glancing down at the silvery threads of semen on his skin. 'Want to lick it off and find out?'

'That's a very kind offer,' I said, 'but no thanks.'

Mark rolled his eyes. 'That's what I thought you'd say. Never mind. Pass me a couple of tissues, will you?'

I reached for the box on the table by the bed, pulling out a handful. 'Lie down,' I told him, 'I'll do it for you.'

He watched me warily, as though wondering what I was up to, and I moved closer. Then he did what he was told and lay back on the bed.

I began mopping up the creamy liquid, getting closer to his penis than ever before, even wiping a drip from the end of it as it began to lose its firmness and droop from the vertical, although I was careful not to touch it with my fingers. But I did allow my fingertips to dip into the warm sticky fluid, examining its texture for a moment before quickly rubbing the stuff off.

Mark folded his arms behind his head, enjoying himself as I cleaned him up. Carefully, I collected as much of his spunk on the thick wad of tissues – which I then smeared all over his smug face!

He shouted out in surprised anger, leaping up and trying to grab me. But I laughed and jumped aside, making for the bedroom door and charging downstairs. Mark was hard on my heels, yelling at me, but I reached the front door and was outside in a moment. I turned, watching him. There was no way he was going to dash naked out of the house after me.

He stood in the hall, his cock swinging slightly from

side to side, and he wiped at his sticky face with the back of his hand.

'It's okay,' I giggled. 'It washes off easily, and it doesn't smell or taste of anything!'

'Just you wait!' he warned, and he half shut the door so he could hide his nude body behind it. Despite his words, he couldn't disguise his smile.

'Thanks for the lesson, Mark,' I said. 'See you later.' Then I waved goodbye and went back home.

Chapter Four

It didn't take long before I became more directly involved in Mark's favourite hobby and lent him a hand . . .

I'd been thinking about it over the previous few days, wondering if I dared; but my mind was made up when the first time we were alone together again happened to be in my bedroom. I was on home territory and so I felt more secure.

We were alone in the house, and as soon as Mark was in my room I took the initiative before my nerve failed. I reached for the zip of his jeans and tugged it down.

'What are you doing?' he asked.

I didn't answer, because it was obvious what I was doing. Mark smiled, liking what was happening and he simply stood where he was as I removed all his clothes. By that time his cock was fully erect, and tentatively I reached for it, cupping the balls in my hand then sliding my fingers slowly up its warm length towards the purple tip.

'Do you want to lie down or stand up?' I asked.

'Uh . . . ?' Mark swallowed. 'You mean you're going to . . . er . . . ?' He couldn't believe his good luck.

He backed towards my bed, and I followed, keeping a grip on his firm flesh. He sat down, then gradually leaned further away until he was lying on his back. I kneeled by his side, feeling the throbbing pulse as the blood sped through his prick, sensing the latent energy, the hidden power like that of some missile which was about to blast off.

'What do I do?' I asked. 'Just rub it up and down like this?' As I spoke, my right hand grasped my prize and began its work, while I leaned across Mark and balanced the weight of my body on my left arm.

'Yeah, that's right,' he told me. 'Only not so hard, don't grip just one place, let your fingers slide up and down on the skin.'

I did as I was told, watching as the glans vanished then reappeared beneath the foreskin.

'And not quite so fast,' Mark warned. 'We're in no hurry, this isn't a race.'

'That better?' I asked.

He half closed his eyes. 'It's fine,' he sighed. 'Just fine. But . . .'

'What?'

'It's a bit dry,' he told me. 'It's better with a bit of lubrication.'

I shook my head gently, grinning. 'I know exactly what you mean. But if you think I'm going to lick it, you've got to be kidding.' I could have spat onto my hand, but I had a better idea. Letting go, I climbed off the bed and walked towards my dressing table.

'Where you going?' Mark asked, a little worried, thinking that I'd abandoned my task.

'Not far.' I picked up the bottle of baby oil and poured some into my hand, then returned and spread it all over his shaft, my fingertips carefully rubbing it onto the glans. I resumed masturbating him, and his knob slid squelchily through my slimy hand.

'Ah!' Mark groaned joyfully. 'That's great. Must be just what a juicy cunt's like.'

'Close your eyes,' I told him, and he obeyed. 'Imagine that it is a cunt, that your cock's sliding deep into a warm tight twat. My warm tight twat. Isn't it marvellous, so nice . . . so fucking magnificent!'

'Yes,' he agreed, 'yes, yes, yes!'

'You're fucking me, Mark. That's what you're doing. My hand or my cunt, it doesn't matter. You're fucking me, fucking me, fucking me. It might even be my mouth. Think of that. Your prick in my mouth. My lips greedily sucking you in, my tongue hungrily licking your shaft. And it's great, isn't it? You taste so good, Mark, so wonderful, and I want more, more, more. You've got to give me more, more, more. I want you to come in my mouth, I want your delicious spunk on my tongue, I want you to squirt your seed down my throat. I want it now, Mark, I want it now. Give it to me. Now, now, now!'

His breath was coming in short bursts, as fast as my hand was pumping his swollen knob – which suddenly erupted with a burst of creamy spunk which shot right over his shoulder. A moment later came a second fountain which splattered onto his chest, followed by a third, a fourth, and a fifth, each one successively weaker and reaching lower down his torso.

And I watched in delighted fascination, because it was me who'd done it – I had the power, I could manipulate both Mark's prick and his mind, making him ejaculate to my command. It was a terrific feeling, and I'd only just begun.

There's no sight in the world to compare with a jutting penis blowing like a geyser. I was enthralled by this dramatic vision from the very first, and I still am.

The last of Mark's come dripped down off my fingers, and I turned my hand towards me and studied it. I was so pleased with what I'd done that I couldn't resist laying my right palm on his stomach, rubbing it into the pool of semen and wiping it all over his body. Not to be outdone, my left hand joined in, also becoming deliciously sticky, spreading the thick warm drops all over Mark's shaft and balls. My hands stroked his entire body until every atom of spunk had been absorbed into his flesh and my fingers.

Mark's cock was still fully erect, seeming to have lost none of its potential, so I simply grabbed hold of it and resumed jerking him off.

'How was that?' I asked.

Mark shook his head as though totally exhausted. 'Not bad for a beginner,' he commented, then he grinned. 'What about you? Can I do it to you?'

'No!' I told him, letting go and moving away.

'Then can I watch you do it to yourself?'

'No!' I repeated, equally as forcefully.

'Okay, okay!' Mark raised his hands in appeasement, and slowly he sat up. 'That was terrific, you know,' he added. 'Absolutely fantastic.'

I nodded, because I knew it was.

Over the next few months I practised even more, and Mark was a willing experimental victim. I perfected my technique, both manual and verbal. Masturbation is more than a physical act, it requires imagination, something to focus upon. Mere unerotic manipulation of his tool wasn't very satisfactory for either of us, although I had to try it out as part of my course of discovery. Under the wrong circumstances a cock could be stroked and stroked until it became sore, the hand worn out, and still there would be no ejaculation, or so Mark told me – although because he had me to do it for him, that was always enough of a turn on.

I became so good at giving him a manual that I could time his climax almost to the exact second. I could bring him nearly to the peak, then with a deft squeeze of my fingers prevent orgasm and have him begging for release. Soon I was able to do this several times in a row, nearly bringing him off but delaying the ultimate satisfaction until his whole body was trembling with unachieved fulfilment. And then when finally I did allow him to come, it would be even more rewarding for him and spectacular to me – his prick hurling out streamers of white juicy spunk.

One time I didn't even touch him, all I did was talk him into orgasm by telling him to shut his eyes and then imagine what I was saying to him was true. It was as though I were hypnotizing him, making up a story in which he became totally involved, talking really dirty and inventing the sexiest situation that my young mind could think of. In retrospect, knowing what I do now, it was all very tame.

It involved one of the sports teachers at school, a lithe blonde in her mid-twenties called Miss White who all the older boys had sexual fantasies about. I invented a tale of how the male teacher who usually took the boys in Mark's class for athletics was away, and so Miss White had been assigned to look after them. During the lesson, I said, Mark hadn't been able to keep his eyes off the woman – the way her breasts bounced inside her track suit top, how her long tanned legs moved as she ran, the way her buttocks filled out her brief shorts which were so tight that they couldn't hide the outline of her cunt.

Even a cold shower after the lesson wasn't enough to dampen Mark's enthusiasm, and he still had an erection when he left the changing room and headed for his next class. But then he noticed he'd forgotten his books, and he went back. They weren't where he'd left them, so he thought the teacher must have found them. He supposed she'd put the books in her room for safety and so he knocked on the door. There was no reply, and when he knocked again the door opened slightly. Mark went inside, and as he did he heard a gush of water coming from a doorway a yard beyond him. Carefully, he peeped around the corner – and he found himself staring at Miss White.

Naked.

In the shower. Her head tilted back and letting the water spray all over her. One hand rubbing at her high shapely breasts and the firm nipples, as big as strawberries and the same colour. The other hand washing her blond pubic hairs. No, not washing, but instead rubbing and rubbing, the fingers sliding between her legs. Masturbating.

I told Mark that he was watching in amazement when suddenly the teacher's eyes opened – and she stared directly at him. She looked surprised for a second, but she neither tried to cover herself nor did

45

she stop what she was doing. Instead, she took her hand away from her wet breasts and beckoned to him. Mark obeyed, as if in a dream finding himself fully dressed under the shower with the superb nude body of the teacher.

She pulled him close, pressing her wet lips against his, kissing him hard while her dexterous fingers began to tear off his clothes until he was as naked as she. Their limbs intertwined as they tumbled to the floor together, the warm water pouring onto their glistening bodies. Miss White's fingers and lips were everywhere, touching and kissing Mark all over his body, her hands finding his hard cock and drawing it into her mouth. They were lying side by side, and her cunt was in front of Mark's mouth, her legs apart, inviting him to savour her twat.

And while the teacher devoured the boy's prick, his lips went to her pink cunt lips, his tongue plunging inside. He licked and sucked while she sucked and licked, and he'd never experienced anything so sensational in his whole life. In a matter of seconds he was ready to climax –

– and as I verbally triggered him, I watched Mark's prick erupt in throw after surging throw. Miss White would have been proud of him, I thought, because his first spurt must have set a new long distance record. I felt a little jealous of the teacher, but I realized my envy was misplaced because it was me who'd talked Mark into orgasm. A new stage in my control of him, and of the male sex.

I'd made it all up from what Mark had told me. I knew as much about sucking as I did fucking, I had a theoretical knowledge but that was all. I was catering to his fantasies, and so it was only natural for him to respond so well when I repeated them to him.

Mark kept talking about me sucking him off, but I had no inclination to give him a blowjob – I didn't want a mouthful of spunk. My main interest was to see his cock begin to spurt and know that it was me,

46

me who was responsible. If it was in my mouth or even my cunt, I wouldn't be able to watch the trails of jism as they jetted through the air.

He also said that he wanted to masturbate me, but I wasn't having that. I'd never let him touch me and I didn't want him to. It was my body, not his, and I wasn't going to share it. We had never even kissed, although we'd come close on a few occasions. When I'd been prepared to let him kiss me, Mark had always shied away as though embarrassed. It was okay for me to jerk him off, but he didn't like the idea of kissing – that was too intimate.

I had tried bringing myself off several times, but never with any great result, so I didn't think Mark would be able to do any better. I achieved more satisfaction from watching him come, because it was then that I felt my cunt become moist and could sense it almost trembling. Mark had also told me everything I knew about my twat, which was clever of him since he'd never seen a real one, only picked up his information from pictures in magazines and reading about them. It was from him that I'd discovered I owned a clitoris, although I wasn't too sure whether I'd been able to find it yet or not.

Equally as often he asked me to take my clothes off so he could look at me, but I always refused. I didn't mind him looking at me from a distance, when he was in his room and I in mine; but my clothes always stayed on while I was manipulating his cock and making him ejaculate.

My bedtime habits hadn't altered. I still undressed with the curtains open and the light on. If Mark was watching, that was okay, it didn't bother me. Sometimes, however, I couldn't resist teasing him. I'd go and stand nude in front of the window and rub my hands across my breasts, then let one of them slide down towards my cunt and pretend that I was finger-fucking myself.

Then one day while jerking Mark off, quite spontaneously I took off my T-shirt and bra. I don't know what prompted me to do it, perhaps it was because I was becoming bored with the same old routine. There has to be a variety in sex, like everything else, if it isn't to become a habit and something which is done out of mere routine.

My boobs had developed a lot over the past year, and I no longer hated them. They weren't too big to be uncomfortable, nor too small as to be not worth having, nicely rounded with pert pink nipples. My hips had also filled out, and the only trace of my once boyish build was in my trim waist and slender limbs. No longer a girl, I was almost a woman.

Mark said nothing, he simply watched as my breasts swayed above him, while my hand resumed its work as skilfully as ever on his stiff member. He didn't try to touch my boobs, because he was aware I wouldn't like it and that as a reprisal I'd pull away and leave him hovering on the brink. I lowered my body across his waist, allowing my nipples to brush against the tip of his glans, and almost immediately he groaned and ejaculated, the first gush of white come arcing up between my breasts, missing them by a fraction of an inch. But when he'd finished spurting, I rubbed my boobs all across his stomach and chest, coating them in the precious sticky fluid.

I learned a lot from Mark, the basis of everything I know about sex; but one of the most important things was that I should never be predictable. There should be something new and unexpected all the time. And everything shouldn't be given at once, there always had to be a reserve – the male must be aware that the female has more to offer, that she is holding back a little and that next time will grant him something extra and make the experience even more sensational.

And so, bit by bit, I offered Mark more of myself. He wanted me as the high priestess in the cult which worshipped his phallus, and that I became – though I never went as far as to kiss his cock or lick his come, I forever kept him hoping. Mark was my initiation into the world of male sex, their desires and lusts. By giving him what he desired, by seeming to obey his every sexual whim, it was I who was secretly in control and he who was my slave. I could twist him around, make him do what I wished while he thought that it was he who held the whip hand.

I had given Mark very little, but he believed I'd let him have everything. One thing he kept pestering me for was my cunt, and because I'd learned and experienced so much through him, I conceded. I finally decided he could have my twat on the same conditions as the rest of me: I'd allow him to look, but no more than that.

'But why not?' he asked me for the umpteenth time, staring at my crotch through my scanty cotton briefs.

I'd gradually been wearing less and less. After being bare-breasted while tossing him off, I'd graduated to doing it while wearing only my panties, sometimes even squatting above him and sliding my flimsily covered cunt across his erection, pinning down his arms above his head with my hands while I brought him to a spurting climax.

This was the closest I could get to actually fucking him, our genitals separated by a thin layer of fabric. But it was time for the ultimate revelation, and so when he came out with his usual rhetorical question, I thumbed down my underwear and stood naked in front of him.

He'd seen me nude many times before, but never so close, and his eyes widened as they gazed at my dark hairy bush.

'Oh, but that's beautiful,' he whispered. He was sitting on the edge of the bed, stripped, waiting for me to service him; his cock seemed to take on greater dimensions than ever before.

I climbed onto the bed, pushing him down with one of my bare feet, and stood astride him, allowing him to stare up into the cleft between my legs as I slowly

49

lowered my cunt towards his face to give him a better view.

Being aware of all the magazines he'd studied so intently, I knew how fascinated he was by the female sex organ. All I had to do was show him my cunt, and he was transfixed, such was my power over him – and my potential domination over every other male I encountered.

Kneeling astride his head, facing towards his legs, I allowed my fingers to slide into the dampness of my vaginal lips, pulling them apart to display the inner labia. And for the first time in ages, Mark couldn't wait. He knew I wouldn't let him touch me, and so he grabbed hold of his prick and began to hurriedly jerk himself off.

I watched as his hand frantically pumped his tool, his hips jerking up and down, the fingers of his right hand working furiously on his shaft while those of his left stroked his balls.

When he came, his come squirted high and straight, splashing against my stomach and trickling down into my pubic hairs. As I massaged the creamy spunk into my flesh, I thought how everything with Mark had been a game. We had only been playing at sex, I still knew very little of the real thing.

I was tiring of Mark as a playmate. I knew his cock and its behaviour perfectly, but Mark was only one man – hardly even a man, just a boy. Like me he was still a virgin.

It was time to move on, to find a new challenge.

Chapter Five

The logical place to start was at school. There were plenty of boys there, and each one of them had what I was interested in – a prick. I'd always been regarded as a tomboy by the others in our class, and so I was an outsider and had no friends amongst either the girls or boys. It hadn't bothered me up until now, but I was determined to change all that.

Most of the other girls always adopted a helpless female role, pretending to be dumb and inferior just so they could attract the boys. All the guys asked of them was a nice smile and a good figure. It was the males who made all the running when it came to picking up girls. Men were the hunters, women the helpless quarry, waiting to be swept off their feet and onto their backs by a tall dark stranger like some damsel in distress.

There was no way I could have changed my nature so quickly. I couldn't be subtle, because the other girls had years of developing and trying out their feminine tactics. All I could do was be bold and direct, and the way to a guy's heart is through his penis.

I used to sit next to a boy called Danny, not through choice but only because he was a loner like me. He had no real friends in class, so whenever it came to pairing off for some project or other we were usually left stuck with each other. Danny was a very quiet boy, and I couldn't blame him for that because he had a stammer which always became much worse whenever he was asked to speak in class. It was so bad that sometimes he could hardly get the words out, and everyone would laugh at him – me too, I'm sorry to admit.

What was worse was that some of the teachers would sadistically pick on him just to amuse the rest of the

51

class. He had bright red hair and a ruddy complexion, so he also blushed very easily. Often his face would go crimson with embarrassment when he was trying to answer a question. He knew the answers, but it took him a long time to spit them out.

He and I got on fairly well together and had developed a mutual understanding. Because we sat at the back of the class, whenever a teacher pointed him out to give a verbal answer I would pretend that I thought it was me who was being questioned and shout out a reply. I didn't usually get it right, but some other smartass would yell out the right answer; like I said, I hated school and couldn't be bothered learning much. In return for helping him out, Danny would let me copy from the notes he made when I was daydreaming and staring out of the window.

I felt sorry for Danny because everyone was so against him. Every class has a scapegoat, and he was ours. If he hadn't been there, it would probably have been me – so I was grateful to him for that.

One day after the geography teacher had called on Danny to give an answer and when I'd been gazing at the ceiling, not paying attention and so not realized, the boy had gone bright red as he finally stammered the reply, and to try to calm him I put my hand on his leg beneath the desk. He stared at me in astonishment, and gently I rubbed at his thigh, smiling at him. He put his hand on top of mine, trying to pull it off, but then I dropped my other hand on top of his.

'Relax,' I whispered. 'Don't let them get to you. Think about something else.' Then I lifted his hand and plonked it on my bare knee, taking away my own hands; and I'd never even let Mark so much as touch me there. Although I used to hate skirts, I wore one at school.

Danny kept gazing at me in amazement, but it took him several seconds before he removed his hand. He gave me a slight smile, and gradually the flush faded from his face.

'You think too much about the question,' I added in a low voice. 'You get all worked up because everyone's listening, and you think that you're going to stammer and go red – and because of that you do stammer and go red. You know all the answers, Danny, you're the cleverest person in the class. And that includes the teacher. So don't bother about them. Think of something else and just answer the question.'

'Th-that's easier f-for you to s-say than m-me,' he replied softly.

'See?' I replied. 'You hardly stammered at all then, because you were only talking to me. When you answer, just pretend there's no one else but me. Just concentrate on me – put your hand on my leg, and think of that.' So saying, I replaced his hand on my leg, higher up my bare thigh.

'What are you two talking about at the back there?' the geography teacher demanded. He was a small skinny runt in his mid-fifties, who knew everything about everywhere in the world – but had spent his whole life in this one town, this one school.

'Nothing,' I said.

The teacher stared at Danny as though I hadn't spoken. 'Well, boy, answer me!'

I put my hand on Danny's, squeezing it, sliding it even higher up my leg, under the hem of my skirt. Whatever happened, at least I was giving him something else to think about.

Danny's mouth opened and his eyes turned towards me, glancing down to where his hand was vanishing under my skirt and then suddenly feeling his fingertips brush against the edge of my panties.

'N-n-nothing!' he blurted out, in about a quarter of the time it usually took him to give an answer.

The teacher stared at him, surprised at the speed of his reply, then turned away. I gave Danny's fingers a squeeze then removed my hand. The boy was watching me, and he shook his head slightly in bewilderment.

Then he realized where his hand was and he slipped it free. I winked at him.

'See?' I said, stunned by the fact that my impromptu theory had succeeded. He just needed confidence, I supposed. I was more confident in my abilities than I'd ever been, and so I was happy to pass some of it on.

During the next break, Danny followed me outside. I recognized the look in his eye, I'd seen it before in Mark. Glancing over my shoulder to show him I knew he was behind me, I walked towards the far end of the new annex and around the corner which led to the gymnasium. Between the two buildings was a dark passage known as 'smoke alley', where often a number of kids could be found having a quick cigarette before the next lesson. There was no one there today, and I walked into the deepest shadows by the far wall.

'Wh-what you d-doing in here?' Danny asked me. 'C-come for a sm-smoke?'

'No,' I answered as I leaned against the brick wall. 'What are you doing here?'

'I f-followed you,' he said, as he stood against the wall by my side so that he wouldn't have to look directly at me. 'I w-wanted to s-say th-thanks.'

'For what? I didn't do anything. I only let you put your hand on my leg, that's no big deal. It was you who answered "nothing" to slime-features.'

'B-b-b-b . . .'

I raised my hand. 'No more of that, Danny. You've got to learn to relax.' I stared at him in the gloom. 'Did you like putting your hand on my leg?'

He shrugged, trying to act nonchalant. 'It w-was o-okay.'

'Have you ever done that before, put your hand on a girl's leg? On her thigh? Touched her panties? Been only an inch or two away from her cunt?'

He didn't answer, and it was obvious that he hadn't.

'You haven't got a girlfriend, have you?' I said.

Danny shrugged.

'You've never had a girlfriend, have you?'

54

He didn't even bother shrugging this time.

'So you've never had a girl do this to you,' I said casually, and I reached across and took hold of the top of his zip and tugged it down.

'Hey!' he said, without a trace of stammer, and his hand went down to seize my wrist.

'Relax, Danny, just relax,' I said. 'How many times do I have to tell you?' I freed my hand with my other one, brushing his arm out of the way, then delving inside his pants, pushing away the bottom of his shirt and the elastic of his underwear until at last I found what I was seeking.

His cock was small and timid, still curled up, and I let it rest in the palm of my left hand while I stroked it to life with the fingers of my right. It didn't take long before it started to respond, swelling and growing and standing erect.

Danny was leaning against the wall, staring down at my hands on his prick as if he didn't know what was happening.

'I just love cocks,' I said to him. 'You masturbate, don't you?'

He shook his head slowly, either in denial or disbelief; if it was the former, I was sure he wasn't telling the truth.

'Is it okay if I jerk you off?' I asked. 'I'm good at it, very good. You'll like it, I'm sure you will.' Even as I spoke, I began to slide my fingers up and down his shaft. His knob was slightly different from Mark's, a little thinner and not quite so long; but right at the moment it was plenty big enough.

It was as if I had Danny bound and gagged, because he neither moved nor spoke as I manipulated his tool, my fingers sliding from the base of his shaft right up to the ridge around his glans.

'You like it?' I asked him.

He managed to nod, his head rocking up and down in the rhythm of my stroke. He kept watching what I was doing, as though this was some kind of test and he had to memorize everything that I did. I became aware that his hips were pushing in and out slightly, aiding the movement as his cock rubbed through my palm.

All the time we were standing side by side, with me on Danny's left and using my right hand to toss him off. I kept an eye out for intruders appearing around the corner. It was dark enough for us not to be seen so far back, and we'd have time to compose ourselves if someone did show up.

But I needn't have worried about that, because Danny came in less than half a minute after I'd begun my task. I heard a gurgling sound in the back of his throat, which was my first clue that he was about to ejaculate. His hands came down, one gripping my wrist and forcing it to halt, the second clutching my hand and clamping it even tighter around his bulging prick as he aimed it away. A second later, a stream of shiny spunk shot from the end of his tool, followed by a diminishing series of squirts which splashed to the ground between the two school buildings.

We returned every day for the rest of the week and found a time when no one else was there, and then I would jerk him off.

The following Monday, during history, I nudged Danny in the ribs. He turned to glance at me, and slowly I slid the hem of my skirt up my thigh, over my hips and almost to my waist. His eyes widened as he noticed I wasn't wearing any panties. I let my skirt fall back into place again, then carried on staring at the teacher as though nothing had happened. I hadn't intended to come to school with nothing beneath my skirt, but when I'd searched for some clean briefs that morning I couldn't find any – so I simply hadn't bothered.

By drawing Danny's attention to my lack of covering I wanted him to anticipate what I might be planning, what I might let him see or do; and all through the lesson he kept on looking at me and whispering – asking if I really didn't have any underwear on, why not, if we were going into smoke alley again during the break.

'Okay, that's enough!' the history teacher suddenly shouted. He pointed accusingly at Danny, then gestured for him to stand, pick up his things off the desk and walk towards the front of the class. 'I've had enough of you talking,' the teacher continued, 'you're going to sit right here where I can keep an eye on you. You two swap places, you go and sit at the back where he was.'

The boy he'd sent to take Danny's place at my side was Martin, who looked very annoyed as he picked up his books and trudged to the back of the room. Martin was the best looking boy in the whole class, and he knew it. He had short fair hair and a long, lean body, and all the girls in the class fancied him. Except me. Or I hadn't . . . until now.

He hardly glanced at me as he sat down, and I pretended to ignore him and carry on writing. But instead of making notes on the lesson, I wrote a note for Martin and slid it across the desk to him.

It said *Can I have a look at your cock?*

He glanced at the folded piece of paper between us, and I turned to watch his expression. Disdainfully, he picked up the note, holding it casually between his fingers for a few seconds as though he was bored and didn't care what it said. When he finally did open it up, he stared in bewilderment as if he couldn't understand the words. Then his expression became one of astonishment, and his eyes were wide and his mouth slightly open as he turned to face me. He shook his head briefly, then glanced away and began tearing the note into tiny unreadable pieces.

Why not? I wrote on another slip of paper. *Is there something wrong with it? Is it so small you're ashamed?*

This time he screwed the paper into a tiny ball, not even looking at me.

The third note read *How can I masturbate you if you don't pull it out?*

He left this piece of paper between us for almost a minute, but finally his curiosity got the better of him and he opened it up. He stared at me again.

I kept my face deadly serious, and I nodded just once before glancing down at his groin. My eyes remained focused there for a long time, during which he shifted his position on the seat, sliding his feet along the floor and straightening his legs. His hands rested on his lap, to cover the growth which I was convinced must have been taking place there.

I started writing again. *Would you like to see my cunt?* I pushed the paper towards Martin, and to prove how serious I was I began to tug the side of my skirt up my thigh and towards my hips, demonstrating my lack of underwear. He couldn't tear his eyes away from the ever increasing expanse of bare white flesh, and I tucked the fabric of my skirt between my legs to prevent too much exposure.

Martin was holding the note between his trembling hands, and he nodded a brief reply. I smiled but shook my head, making a gesture at my crotch as though I was pulling down a zip.

The boy licked at his lips, reluctantly turning his attention away from me and looking around the class. The teacher was reciting, and everyone else was quickly copying down his immortal words. Hesitantly, Martin's hands touched the top of his zip, then he pulled away, shaking his head.

I pretended to jerk off an imaginary cock growing from between my legs, while my other hand stroked my bare thigh. Before Martin could respond, the bell rang to signal the end of the lesson. I sighed, then swiftly flipped up my skirt and gave the boy the briefest flash of my pubic curls. He groaned, his hand grasping at the bulge in his pants, and for a moment I thought he'd creamed himself.

It was break time, and I led him deep into smoke alley and leaned against the wall, saying nothing, waiting for him to extract his prick. He knew this was what I wanted, and finally he unzipped himself. His prick was hard and pink as I took it in my hand and began to stroke it up and down.

'Does Sarah do this for you?' I asked him. Sarah was one of the girls in our class, a small girl with enormous breasts, and she and Martin had been going out together recently – and they gave each other big purple love bites on the neck for the rest of the class to see.

Martin shook his head, already beginning to breathe faster.

'Why not?' I asked. 'That's not very friendly of her. Does she let you touch her?'

'A little bit,' he replied, his eyes gazing down as my fist slid expertly along his shaft.

'Have you touched her breasts?'

'Yes.'

'What about her nipples? Have you touched her nipples?'

Martin shook his head.

'But you must have seen them,' I said. 'What are her nipples like? Are they big, like her tits?'

'I don't know,' Martin managed to say, 'I haven't seen them.'

'Haven't seen them?' I repeated. 'But you said you'd touched her breasts.'

'Only through her clothes,' he admitted.

I almost laughed. Martin and Sarah pretended that they were having a passionate romance, and he'd never even got inside her bra!

'What about her cunt?' I asked. 'You can't have seen her cunt or even touched it.'

He didn't reply, and my hand became still.

'No,' he said immediately. 'I haven't seen it, haven't touched it.'

59

'Sarah's not nice to you, is she? Not as nice as me?' I gave his prick an extra squeeze to encourage a reply.

'No, she's not nice,' he answered. 'Not as nice as you.'

'You've already glimpsed my cunt, Martin,' I said to him. 'And if you're really good, if you can shoot off lots of nice creamy spunk, maybe I'll let you have a better look. Perhaps you can even touch it. Would you like that?'

'Oh,' he muttered, 'oh, oh, oh, oh, oh . . . !' As he moaned, his dick began to splash the ground with jets of come.

I rubbed my fingers over the glans to wipe off the last drips, then held them up to his face.

'You've made my hand all sticky, Martin,' I complained. 'I think you ought to lick it off.'

He shook his head quickly.

'I think you should,' I told him quietly, 'or there may not be a next time. And if Sarah doesn't masturbate you, that means you'll have to do it all by yourself. And that isn't so good, is it?'

He closed his eyes, moving his face towards my hand, and obediently he licked my fingertips, sucking hungrily at every last drop of his come. As he did so, I became aware that we weren't alone – another dim figure had entered the passage and was watching us.

I recognized who it was, and I beckoned to him with my free hand.

'Hey, Danny!' I called. 'Over here. It's your turn . . .'

Chapter Six

I suppose it was only to be expected that there was no way the boys could keep such a good thing to themselves, and by the end of the month I'd wanked every one of them . . . and also become the most popular girl in class. The other girls knew something was going on but couldn't quite work out what it was.

Word spread, and soon I was masturbating guys from other classes and years. I asked nothing in return because I enjoyed it tremendously, revelling in the pints of spunk which I'd conjured up. Smoke alley was almost literally awash in a sea of semen. My main rule was that no one could touch me, I was the one who did the touching – and anyone who tried otherwise was no longer jerked off. I was outnumbered by the boys, and had they wanted they could have forced themselves upon me; but I was aware that couldn't happen while I maintained control.

I wasn't doing it all the time; I didn't have them queueing up or anything like that. But gradually over the weeks I notched up a bigger score.

Then the inevitable happened: I was caught.

The teachers would occasionally check on smoke alley to ensure no one was smoking. It never occurred to them that it might be used for another purpose. I'd been lucky that I hadn't been found out before, but at last I was caught sticky handed.

I was with another two boys from my class, Tommy and Roger, one hand firmly wrapped around each of their tools. It was a bit of an experiment. I'd jerked off two guys at a time before, but here I'd been trying to bring them to a simultaneous climax and so had failed to notice the burly figure of Mr Carter, one of the chemistry teachers, as he strode towards us.

'What the hell's going on here!' he yelled, which was the first warning we had of his presence.

Immediately I let go of my captive cocks. Roger spun around, trying to tuck his prick back inside his pants. But it was too late for Tommy, whose knob began to spray spunk all around as he attempted to turn away.

The teacher came to a halt, watching in absolute amazement. He opened his mouth, but no words emerged for a few seconds. There was no way we could escape, he had us trapped.

'What are you doing?' he asked eventually, which I thought was a stupid question because it was obvious what we'd been doing.

'Revising for the exams,' I said.

'Don't be so insolent, girl!' Mr Carter proclaimed, reaching out to grab Tommy and Roger by the scruffs of their neck so he could spin them around and see who they were. 'I want you two outside the chemistry lab after school. Now get out of here!' He almost picked them up and threw them back down the passageway.

Then he turned on me. 'As for you,' he hissed, 'you little whore . . .'

I tried to look puzzled. 'Whore?' I said, and I shook my head. 'I don't think so, sir. Doesn't a whore do it for money?' I gazed innocently up at him.

He glared at me, unable to think of a reply.

I glanced along the passage. Tommy and Roger had disappeared, and no one else would be coming because the word would have spread that there was a teacher around.

'There's no one here now, sir,' I said. 'Would you like me to show you what I was doing? I was masturbating them. I'm very good at it. I can do it for you if you want, sir.' I took a step towards the teacher, my hand stretching out as though reaching for his zip.

The man scowled me and instantly he raised his arm, pulling it back for a slap then bringing it down hard and fast towards me. I didn't flinch, and at the last moment he drew back his open palm and let his hand fall.

'And I want you, girl,' he said quietly, 'also outside the chemistry lab after school. You hear?'

'Yes, sir,' I said politely.

Then he turned on his heel and stormed away.

And so after classes were over that day I stood waiting for him. Tommy and Roger were outside the lab, but they wouldn't meet my eye. It was as though we were there for completely different reasons, that I was in no way connected with the offence for which they'd been summoned. I didn't care. If they wanted to play it that way, it was fine by me. I leaned against the opposite wall and ignored them, hardly even noticing when Mr Carter called them in. Ten minutes later they left. I didn't bother looking at them, and then it was my turn to enter the small office behind the laboratory.

'Okay, girl,' he demanded, closing the door behind me, 'what have you got to say for yourself?'

I shrugged. 'What do you want me to say? We weren't doing any harm, quite the opposite. We were all enjoying ourselves until you came along.'

'Oh, so I'm a spoilsport?' The man shook his head, staring at me. He wasn't much taller than me, although very broad. His hair was short and dark, and so was his beard. He was probably about thirty, although that seemed ancient to me.

'We can't have this, you know,' he continued. 'Pubic masturbation during school hours. Next thing we know you'll be . . .' He broke off. 'You're a bad influence, girl, that's the story I've heard. What do you say about that?'

'Me?' I asked in surprise. 'Why blame me? They weren't my cocks. All I did was –'

The chemistry teacher interrupted me before I could finish. 'I know exactly what you did, girl.' he said coldly, 'and there's a time and place for everything. I could understand it if you were doing that to your boyfriend – but I hear you do it for everyone.'

I considered telling him they were all my boyfriends, but I didn't. 'That's right,' I agreed. 'I don't play favourites.' I stared at his crotch. 'What I said earlier, it still goes. Do you fancy it? Can I jerk you off, sir?'

'Don't play games with me, girl,' he warned.

'I'm not playing, sir. There's just you and me here, who's to know? I won't tell anyone, and I know you'd like it. Are you married, sir? Does your wife masturbate you?'

'Shut up!' Mr Carter ordered.

'Or does she just let you fuck her in the dark, once a month while she lies on her back not moving? I bet she doesn't let you stick your cock in her mouth. Does she suck the end of your knob between her lips and lick it for you, then let you come all over her face, sir?'

The teacher glanced away from me, staring up at the ceiling and trying to lose neither his temper nor his patience. 'I don't know what you're trying to do, girl,' he said very slowly, 'whether to annoy me or turn me on, but I assure you this language of yours is doing you no good whatsoever.'

'How long since you saw a juicy young cunt, sir?' And so saying, I raised my skirt above my waist.

Recently I'd got into the habit of not wearing any panties because I liked the way the air blew through the lips of my cunt – and I enjoyed the way I could surprise and shock people by giving them a quick flash of my bushy triangle. There was a school rule about the older girls having to wear a bra all the time, probably because they didn't want the male teachers to be distracted by so many ripe teenage bouncing boobs. But it was easy to get away with not wearing briefs, because there was no way anyone could tell – unless I wanted them to . . .

The man gazed at me, his eyes focused directly on my twat as I spread my legs a few inches wider.

'I think you're one of the worst pupils I've ever

encountered in my teaching career,' he told me. 'You're rude, you're insolent, you're disobedient. I was wondering earlier how I could punish you properly, but now I know. It's very old fashioned, and not many people in the profession would approve – but as you so aptly pointed out, we're alone in here and who will know?'

As he spoke, he unbuckled the thick leather belt around his waist, pulling it free then snapping it in the air like a whip. He smiled without a trace of humour. I let my skirt fall in to place, and I backed away but my retreat was blocked by his desk. I leaned against it, beginning to feel scared; I didn't like the idea of being hurt.

'It's between you and me, girl,' said the teacher. 'We can get this over and done with now, or else I can report it to the headmaster. That way soon the whole school will know and your parents will find out. So what's it to be? That? Or me?'

I licked at my dry lips and managed to nod. 'You,' I said quietly.

'All right.' Mr Carter locked the door and stepped closer towards me. 'Turn around,' he ordered. 'Lean across the desk.'

I did as I was told.

'Spread your legs wider,' he commanded, 'you're too high.'

I obeyed, bending double and stretching over the desk top.

'Now raise your skirt,' the teacher added.

I lifted the hem of my skirt, pulling it up around my waist. Then I waited for the leather strap across my bare buttocks, my eyes closed and my teeth gritted in awful anticipation. Why was he taking so long and prolonging the agony? I wanted him to start and get it over with as soon as possible.

Then finally I felt something, and instantly I winced and cried out at the sudden contact; but then I realized that what I'd felt across my backside wasn't a leather strap.

It was warm, fleshy, pressing against both of my buttocks – the man's naked thighs! He'd dropped his pants and was right behind me, forcing something through my legs, up against my cleft, rubbing against my labia.

And it didn't take much of a guess to know that it was his hard cock . . . !

I gasped as he rubbed his glans against my cunt lips, my whole body tingling. I could have slid away, escaped, but that wasn't what I wanted. Because what I wanted, and what I needed, was the teacher's prick inside me. He was a man, not a boy, and my first fuck had to be a good one, from a guy who knew what he was doing. This was why I'd teased him earlier, even though my reasons had been subconscious, now it all made sense.

The tip of his knob glided through my labia, sending shivers of delight through every nerve, gently rubbing and rubbing, filling me with lust and desire. I sensed my twat becoming moist, twitching open and waiting for his prick to force its way into my untouched cunt.

'Hurry up,' I sighed. 'Do it. Do it to me.'

'Do what?' asked Mr Carter, as though he was conducting an experiment in his chemistry laboratory.

'Fuck me!' I cried. 'Fuck me, sir! Fuck me, please!'

And then he slid the end of his prick gently into me, the glans massaging the walls of my vulva as I squeezed my cunt muscles to take a tighter grip on his shaft. And I shuddered rapturously.

He began to fuck me, his cock slipping in and out, slowly at first, then working up speed. Faster and faster, deeper and deeper came the thrusts. I could feel his hands under my torso, pulling me up off the desk, tearing at the buttons of my blouse and ripping the garment away before tearing off my bra. His hands found my breasts, cupping them in his palms while the fingers worked on the hardness of my nipples to further increase my almost unbearable pleasure.

I had never imagined it might be so wonderful, couldn't possibly have suspected that contact with another body would be so splendid – and this was just the beginning. The more he fucked me, the greater the sheer bliss which radiated from my cunt and suffused my entire being. I could feel something developing within me, a kind of tension which welled up and was searching for release, growing stronger and more powerful every second. If it didn't find an exit soon, I sensed that I would burst.

I groaned and sighed in joy, my hands reaching out to clutch the man's taut buttocks and urge him deeper into me – and then suddenly, without warning, the whole universe exploded in a cataclysm of rainbow light and a whirlwind crescendo of sound.

I screamed till my lungs were empty, my whole body drained, as I experienced my first shattering orgasm. I felt exhausted, totally weak, but it was a wonderful feeling.

It was called ecstasy.

Only gradually did I recover, but the man was still pumping away into me, changing his rhythm and depth and angle all the time. He'd been fucking me far longer than I'd wanked any boy. But this was why I'd needed him, because any boy would have spunked into my twat long before I was ready for my own climax.

Slowly I realized that the same flow was building up inside me again, only a few waves at first but then magnifying until it became a surging tide which threatened to drown all my senses once more. I was about to have a second orgasm.

But then the instrument of my pleasure was hurriedly withdrawn, sliding from my cunt. The man had pulled out, leaving me hovering on the verge of a climax. That was all that mattered, I didn't care why he'd stopped fucking me – only that he had. His hands had also left my breasts, which they had been massaging so expertly all the time.

As I started to turn, wondering where he had gone, he walked around the side of the desk, his cock held in one hand. I gazed at his prick, all slimy with my cunt juice. It was sturdy and fat, far wider than any I'd encountered previously – but it was a man's penis, not a boy's, and had I seen it before it had fucked me, I'd have thought it too big, that it would have ripped me in half.

All this flashed through my mind in a split second. I had started to rise, but then the teacher's other hand was on the back of my head. His cock was coming closer to my face, and his hand pushed me nearer to the shining purple glans.

Instinctively, I opened my mouth. His cock slid in through my lips and I could taste the tangy flavour which came from deep within my own cunt. The man thrust his hips forward, his prick slipping even further into my mouth while my tongue caressed the glorious offering he'd given me.

Then I felt the shaft tremble against my lips as it began to throb with vitality, and my mouth became filled with warm spunk.

As I felt his jism squirt against the roof of my mouth, savouring its indescribable taste on my tongue, I peaked again, my whole body quivering. My jaw fell open as I gasped for air and cried out in triumph, drops of semen escaping from my lips and dripping down my chin.

I found that knowing Mr Carter was a better way of solving my homework problems than having Mark help me with it – I simply didn't do any for him. The only extra time I spent was after lessons, when he'd lock the door to his room and fuck me like crazy. In a way, while I stayed late in school I was still learning . . .

and what I was taught was far more useful and interesting and enjoyable than my other classes.

I tried to ration the chemistry teacher to one evening a week, because there were others who gave me homework as well and I had to attend to their needs, too. Before long, I had to restrict my extra lessons with my original tutor to once a fortnight.

The word spread amongst the teachers about my extra-curricular activities almost as fast as it had done amongst the boys in school. It was lucky that half of my regular teachers were women, otherwise I'd never have been able to cope. But by spending ten to thirty minutes of my time, three or four times a week, I had the rest of the evenings and weekends free. Letting them fuck me in exchange for not having to do homework was a bargain so far as I was concerned. And I never had to worry about exams any more. I could just sit and stare out of the window, or else draw doodles all over my papers, and I was sure to pass.

If ever I had any doubts, all I'd do was write a short essay reminding the teacher in question of the last time I'd seen him – or telling him what I planned to let him do to me during our next encounter – and that was enough to ensure a high mark.

It amazed me the variations between cocks, that they could be as different as they were. I guess it was like noses, of which there are so many types. But cocks could be fat or thin, short or long or even massive; and there were so many combinations of shapes and sizes, there could hardly have been two the same alike, they were like fingerprints. Some were so big when limp but didn't inflate at all upon erection, while ones no bigger than the last two joints of my little finger could swell to amazing dimensions. There were ones which hung to the left or the right, and the English teacher's prick was as bent as a banana – and that was what I always liked to pretend it was, wriggling my tongue between the foreskin and his glans as he achieved a hard-on.

They all had different preferences when it came to fucking. The oldest was Mr Smeath, who was almost near retirement, and he preferred me to lie on the ground beneath him while he fucked me in the missionary position. That was the way he must have been doing it all his life, and whenever I suggested anything different he wouldn't hear of it. He seemed to think that some of my ideas were disgusting, which I couldn't quite understand. He had two standards: straight screwing was acceptable; anything else he considered weirdly freakish.

Speaking of which, at the opposite end of the scale was Mr Allen, who was in his first year as a teacher, and he could never come unless he piled his clothes on top of my face so he couldn't see me, while his cock pumped away between my boobs. It seemed such a waste of both his chubby knob and his come.

But as I swallowed the other teachers' spunk or my cunt drained their pricks dry, I began to regret all the semen which I'd let pass uselessly through my hands until then. That had all belonged to the boys, however, and the longer I associated with mature men the more I appreciated them. They knew how to treat a girl. There were some who were happy just to shove their cocks in me, slide them up and down, then ejaculate; but they were the exception, and if they treated me like that then it was the last time I let them screw me. It was as though they were simply using me to masturbate – and I'd been through enough of that; my hand was for jerking off, the rest of me was for fucking.

It was on a Tuesday that disaster struck. I can remember that it was a Tuesday because the last lesson was biology, and the teacher had once joked that he'd learned more about biology from me than he had during three years of university. I was sitting nude on his lap at the time, his cock embedded deep in my throbbing twat. An unmarried man in his late twenties

70

and comfortably plump, his name was Mr Compton. I always called the teachers 'Mr' because I'd have felt uncomfortable using their first names.

I had an appointment for another session with Mr Compton after school, and so I remained behind after class until all the others had gone. Then we went through into the small office behind the biology lab, and he closed and locked the door, putting the key in his jacket pocket which he hung over a hook on the wall. When he'd done this, I stripped off for him.

If I was in a hurry, I could peel out of all my school clothes in under ten seconds. But the biology teacher didn't like me to rush. He enjoyed watching me slowly reveal my body to him, and I imagined that I was doing a striptease, even though my garments weren't at all suited to a glamorous, tantalizing unveiling.

But I did my best, slowly unbuttoning my blouse then coyly turning my back on him as I shed it, reaching behind me to unhook my bra and letting it slide off my shoulders, holding my breasts as I turned to face him, gradually spreading my fingers so that my firm pink nipples peeked out, finally dropping my hands away so that he could see my bare boobs, suddenly spinning around and around on my toes, my skirt swirling higher and higher to reveal my bare buttocks and more importantly my uncovered cunt. Then I unhooked my skirt and let it fall, standing naked in front of him except for my shoes and the long woollen stockings which clung all the way up my legs, reaching halfway up my thighs.

After that, I always had to undress him.

'Come on, Mr Compton,' I said, my fingers undoing the knot in his tie. 'You're a big boy now, you ought to be able to take your own clothes off.'

Discarding his tie, I undid all the buttons of his shirt, tugging it loose from his belt and then carefully folding it over the back of the chair.

'We mustn't get it crushed, must we, Mr Compton?' I said to him. 'Then it will need ironing, and I'm

71

certainly not going to iron it for you, so you'd have to do it all by yourself.'

I glanced down at his feet and sighed. 'Can't you even take your own shoes off? Do I have to do everything for you, Mr Compton?'

So saying, I bent down to unfasten his laces, noticing as I did so the prominent bulge in his pants, where his prick was already rising towards the vertical.

'Your shoes are very dirty, Mr Compton,' I chided. 'You haven't been cleaning them lately. You're a very naughty boy. If you don't clean your shoes, I might have to spank you.'

I was never sure what sort of role it was I'd adopted towards the man, something between a nurse, a mother and a teacher. Whatever it was, he liked it – and I liked his cock – so that was the main thing.

I removed his shoes and then his socks, grimacing and wrinkling my nose.

'Mr Compton, you are a dirty boy. I don't think you've washed your feet today.'

He hung his head in shame and chewed at his lower lip. 'I'm sorry,' he muttered.

'So you should be,' I told him. 'You mustn't let it happen again.' I stood up, reaching for the buckle of his belt. 'And what about your little penis, Mr Compton? I hope you've given it a wash.' I began to unzip him. 'You know I only like it when it's clean. I won't let you put it in my mouth unless it's ever so clean.'

'It is,' he assured me, as his pants dropped to the floor.

'That's what you say,' I said doubtfully. 'Let's take a look. I see you've got clean underwear on, Mr Compton, that's a good sign.' But he didn't have it on for long, because I tugged at the waistband, pulling the elastic out to lift it over the man's thrusting erection. 'Oh, Mr Compton! You are rude. Now just you put your penis down. It isn't nice to show it me like that, is it? It's so big, so hard, so virile . . . Why, it's enough to shock any young girl and make her faint. Are you going to let it stay like that and embarrass me?'

'There's only one way to make it go down,' the teacher told me.

'What's that?' I asked innocently, gazing down at his rampant tool.

'It has to be exercised,' he replied. 'It has to be worn out, exhausted.'

'How do we do that, sir?'

'I'll show you.'

It was while he was showing me that it happened.

He was lying across his desk, and I was sitting above him, sliding up and down as I rode his prick, my pulse and breath working treble time, almost ready to climax. We'd been there for several minutes, teasing one another with various kinds of foreplay, until I'd finally impaled myself upon his thick weapon. We'd been making so much noise as our bodies slapped wetly against each other and we panted and groaned in harmony, that neither of us heard anyone outside.

The first I knew was when the door suddenly burst open and three people were standing there, watching us. The back of the teacher's head was towards the door, but I was facing it.

'What's the matter?' the man asked desperately. 'Don't stop. I'm going to come!'

I'd become frozen, his prick embedded in me. I don't know who was the most surprised, me or the three people standing in the doorway. The caretaker, with his hand still on the key with which he'd unlocked the door; the headmaster; the junior biology teacher, Miss Williams.

Mr Compton twisted his head around, following the direction of my stunned gaze, but his hips kept on rhythmically thrusting against mine. He saw the intruders at the same moment he ejaculated; but I'd suddenly lost all my desire. I wasn't used to being under observation while fucking.

I made the first move, climbing off the supine teacher

and stepping down to the ground. A trickle of spunk fell from my cunt and splashed onto the floor.

It turned out that Miss Williams was engaged to Mr Compton. She'd come to see the man and heard us screwing in the office but had taken all the groans and sighs as a sign that he was having a heart attack, and she'd summoned help. From her expression, it seemed that she'd have preferred him to have had a heart attack rather than allow him to fuck me.

Needless to say, I was expelled from school. If I'd realized that would happen, I'd have made my exploits with the teaching staff common knowledge much sooner. I half wondered if perhaps the headmaster was jealous because he was one of the few adult males in the school who hadn't had the pleasure of my cunt.

I never found out what happened to Mr Compton, and neither did I really care. All that bothered me was that I'd fucked him to orgasm, but I hadn't come myself. When I got home, I had to use my fingers to bring myself off.

Chapter Seven

While all this had been going on, I still hadn't fucked Mark. But by now, however, he'd found another girl. Maybe she wanked him off, or perhaps she even let him screw her, I couldn't tell – whenever they were up in Mark's room, he was careful to close the curtains and block off my view.

Although I was curious to know what they got up to, I didn't mind too much, because by then I had a proper boyfriend of my own.

His name was Jerry, and he was a couple of years older than me. He'd already left school, and so he wasn't aware of the reputation I'd won amongst the senior boys. I liked him a lot, because he treated me just like an innocent young girl – he'd take me out to see a film, and we'd sit and watch the movie, just holding hands, then he'd take me home and kiss me goodnight. At first they were just soft gentle kisses, and gradually he worked up the courage to slip his tongue into my mouth. He never tried to touch my breasts, and my cunt must have seemed like forbidden territory to him.

It was strange to have such a relationship at the same time as I was fucking half the teachers in school. Jerry was the innocent one; I was convinced that he'd never fucked, or else he would have been more confident and far less nervous. I longed for his cock, but I enjoyed the deliciously masochistic torture of denying myself his body. I didn't want to make the wrong move. I was letting him make all the play. Often I considered suddenly unzipping him and pulling out his dick, going down on my knees and greedily slurping at his knob. I wondered what his reaction would have been.

Amazement at first, of course; but after that he'd have adored it.

Yet I was determined to wait, because it would have shattered all his illusions about me. It was nice to play a naïve young virgin. Sooner or later he'd make his first blatantly sexual move, and we'd take it from there. Until then it was pleasant to experience an old fashioned boy meets girl romance.

I'd met him through working. I was still at school but had a job on Saturdays to make some extra spending money. I worked as a waitress lunchtimes and evenings in one of the restaurants in the centre of town. Jerry worked there, too, because his father owned the place; his parents had divorced a couple of years back, after his mother had left home for another man.

There'd been no trouble persuading Edward, that was Jerry's father, to hire me. When I went along for the job, I wore my shortest skirt and a blouse from which my boobs were almost bursting free – unlike school, there was no rule at the interview that a bra had to be worn. That way he could tell that I was perfectly qualified and would amply fill a waitress uniform.

We had to wear brief flared skirts, a shoulderless blouse, mesh stockings, high-heeled shoes, and a silly bow tie around our necks. All these were in black, the only white being our thick frilly panties which were all on display as we leaned across the tables, and the tiny hats perched on our heads. I sometimes thought that the main idea was that the customers should be watching us all the time, then they wouldn't notice what they were eating or the size of their bill.

'The pay isn't so good, but you can make it up with tips,' said Helen, the girl who showed me the ropes the first day. 'Remember the motto – big tips for big tits!' Then she'd stared at my deep cleavage and added: 'You should do well here.' We'd both laughed.

I looked very grown up in my uniform, and throughout the first Saturday I'd been aware of Jerry watching me all the time. He was the assistant chef, small with jet black hair, but he was shy, and wouldn't meet my eye. Whenever I glanced at him, he'd look away and pretend he hadn't been staring at me.

After the last of the customers had gone that night, I walked past him to the girls' room to get changed. I was all alone in there, and I heard him follow me down the steps. Pretending not to be aware of him, I decided to give him a thrill, and so I stripped off my uniform and stood naked with my back to him as I went through a charade of searching through my bag; raising one leg to support the bag, leaning over it so that he'd glimpse the profile of my left breast. I slowly turned around, glancing down at the floor, giving him a proper look at my breasts and pubis. Then I looked up – and realized I'd made a mistake.

It wasn't Jerry standing there, it was his father!

Edward grinned at my surprised expression, which I didn't have to fake. I spun around, leaving just my buttocks on display.

The man laughed. 'Don't worry about it,' he said. 'Seen one naked girl, you've seen 'em all!'

I wasn't worried, though I thought it would be best if I pretended to be embarrassed. Still with my back to him, I hurriedly pulled on my jeans and sweatshirt. Then I turned, glaring at him.

'What do you want?' I demanded.

'I just came to say you did well today, that's all, and that I'll call a taxi to take you home if you're ready.' He paused, looking me up and down. 'Or I could give you a lift, I suppose.'

I shrugged. It had been arranged that he would pay my fare home at night. So long as I got back one way or another, I didn't really care. I felt pretty tired after so many hours on my feet, taking orders, carrying in meals, dealing with the customers.

'The most important thing,' Edward added, 'is that

I've got your pay here. Do you want me to give it you now?'

I pretended not to understand the double meaning of his remark, and I nodded. 'Yes, please.'

'I do like a girl who says "please",' the man said, and his eyes surveyed my body again. Then he turned as he heard more footsteps coming down the stairs, and the other three waitresses appeared. They looked at him, looked at me, then looked at him again. 'Just came to give her her pay, girls,' he said hurriedly, passing me an envelope, then retreating the way he'd come.

'Was he bothering you?' asked Helen, glancing up the stairs to make sure Edward had gone before she began to remove her uniform.

I shook my head. 'No,' I told her. 'He only came to give me my money. He seems a very nice man.'

'Oh, he is, he is,' said Helen, and the other two girls laughed briefly. 'He thinks that because we work for him, that he owns us. Just play it cool. Don't let the work get on top of you, and don't let the boss get on top of you either!'

I grinned, although I was thinking how I wouldn't have minded letting Edward have at least one fuck; he was more fanciable than some of the teachers at school that I allowed to screw me. As the other girls got changed, I watched them. They were all between twenty and twenty-five years old, and this was the first time I'd seen any naked women. There's been girls at school, in the showers, but I'd hardly taken any notice of them.

As I saw the lovely nude curves of Helen and Kathy and Petra, I could feel my pulse beginning to increase, sweat to form on my skin and a familiar aching feeling in my cunt – it was almost as though I was watching a man, staring at his hard cock and knowing he was going to fuck me. Their bodies were just so beautiful, so soft and round, that I had to restrain myself from reaching out to touch Petra's uptilted breast with its

78

firm dark nipple, Kathy's magnificently muscled rump, or the soft ginger hairs of Helen's twat.

'Got a boyfriend?' Petra asked me, hiding away her boobs behind a skimpy black bra.

I shook my head.

'Really?' said Kathy, glancing at me. 'A pretty girl like you? I don't know what's wrong with the boys of today.'

'I don't go out with boys,' I told them flatly, and they all stared as though there was something wrong with me. 'I prefer to stay in with them,' I added, and they all laughed.

'Did you notice the way Jerry was looking at you?' Helen asked me. 'He's a good looking boy, you could do a lot worse. I wouldn't mind him putting his finger in my pie.'

'Helen!' warned Kathy, and I noticed her eyes directed at me.

Because I was younger than they were and had admitted not having a boyfriend, they automatically assumed that I was a complete novice when it came to sex. I longed to tell them of my exploits at school, just to shock them and observe their reaction, but it was best if I didn't. They'd take it as boasting. Although I'd overheard them talking about sex, making references to the male customers and the potential size of their penises, or comparing notes about their current lovers, it seemed they remained faithful to one guy at a time. If they knew I was so voraciously amoral, I could well imagine that they would have treated me very badly to cover up for their jealousy. And it would have been jealousy, because how could any girl be satisfied with one man, one prick?

Women need far more sex than any man, as is proved by the length of time in which it takes a female to reach orgasm. I've often thought that I could make three men come before I was even warmed up. All a girl needs a guy for is his knob, and once he'd spunked and couldn't keep it up any more he was useless to her.

I'd probably had more lovers than any one of them; but it was always the best policy to keep my mouth shut unless I had to. There were only three reasons for a girl opening her mouth: To eat and drink: to ask a question or say something worthwhile; and to further her skills in the exquisite art of fellatio.

When they were all dressed, they went back upstairs. Because they worked at the restaurant full time, they'd been paid the previous day. The guy Petra lived with was picking her up, and also giving Helen a lift home. There was a taxi for Kathy who lived on the other side of town, in the opposite direction to me. And Edward was standing with his set of car keys in his hand. He glanced at the other three girls, then said: 'Jerry will give you a lift, if that's okay.'

I told him it was, then I said goodnight to the other three waitresses and added that I'd see them next week. Jerry led me out to his father's car, unlocked the passenger door and held it open for me, then drove me home. He didn't say a word until he arrived outside my house, and neither did I.

I knew that he wanted to say something, so I didn't open the door and climb out; I just waited. He was staring at me from the corner of his eye, and after a few seconds he switched the engine off.

'Er . . .' he began, and I turned towards him with an encouraging smile. 'Is this where you live?'

'That's right.'

He nodded. 'Good, good. Er . . .'

'Yes?' I prompted.

'Did everything go okay today?'

'Fine,' I assured him.

'Then you'll be back next week?'

'Yes, why not?'

'Sometimes we have girls who only come once,' Jerry said, 'then they never show up again. I hope that that won't happen to you.'

'I'll be there next Saturday.'

I noticed him lick at his lips. This was it, I realized, now or never.

'What about before then are you doing anything on Thursday that's my night off I thought maybe we could go out,' he said very rapidly.

'That sounds great,' I told him. 'Thursday? No I'm not doing anything, Jerry. I'd like to go out with you. Anywhere in particular?'

He stared blankly at me as though he hadn't understood what I'd said. Then his expression changed to wide-eyed amazement, as if he couldn't believe that I'd agreed to go out with him.

'Er . . .' was all he could say.

'You can decide during the week where we're going,' I said, or else we'd have sat there all night. 'Why don't you come and pick me up at half past seven?'

Jerry nodded. 'I'll pick you up at half past seven,' he told me.

'That's a good idea,' I agreed, and I smiled again. 'I'll look forward to it.' I sat waiting for Jerry to open the car door for me, and finally he did, when it had properly sunk in that he'd really dared to ask me for a date and I'd actually agreed.

The following Thursday he took me to the movies, and we sat near the front and watched the screen. And that was how he became my first, and only, true 'boyfriend' – because although he was older than me, Jerry was still just a boy. I could tell right from the beginning that it was going to take a long time before we ever got around to fucking.

The Thursday after that he took me out again, but by that time I'd already begun screwing his father.

When the restaurant had closed after lunch on my second Saturday there, I was the last one left in the girls' room because I'd started flicking through a magazine I found in there, then become interested in one of the articles and hardly realized what the time

81

was. The other three girls had already left, gone shopping in town until they were due back for when the restaurant opened in the evening.

I made my way up the stairs, thinking how strange it was for the place to be so empty and quiet; but as I reached the kitchen I realized that I wasn't alone. Edward was working at the big table in the centre, dressed in a chef's outfit, surrounded by bowls of flour and cream and fruit and chocolate.

I halted as I saw the man, watching as he sprinkled the work surface with flour and began to roll out a huge lump of pastry. Although I kept completely silent, abruptly he spun around, sensing I was there.

'You!' he sighed, putting his hand on his heart and pretending to let his knees go all weak. 'You gave me a start, I thought everyone had gone. What are you doing here?'

'I was just leaving,' I told him, walking closer. 'What are you making?'

'Oh, nothing much,' he answered. 'Just some cakes.'

'You have to make cakes?' I asked.

'I don't have to,' he said. 'but I started out as a chef and I like to keep my hand in. I'm a master chef, a patissier, and I used to be quite famous in my own small way.'

I nodded, encouraging him to continue.

'It was my ambition to establish a restaurant for gourmets,' he added, 'where people would come for miles to sample the best cooking, a menu offering delicacies from all over the globe. But this place!' He threw up his flour-coated hands in despair. 'All the customers want are steaks, steaks, and more fucking steaks. Excuse my language. That isn't cooking. It's Neanderthal! Cut off a slice of mammoth and throw it on the fire.' He shrugged. 'But we all have to make compromises, you'll discover that as you get older. It's a living, so who am I to complain?'

'Can I help you?' I asked. I didn't particularly want to have to go and wander around town for a couple of hours; I'd only end up buying something I didn't really need or want.

Edward shook his head slightly. 'No thanks, I can manage. I don't like having women in my kitchen, even ones as pretty as you. All the best chefs are men.'

'But women do the cooking in most homes,' I pointed out.

The man shrugged. 'I believe there's only one place for a woman, and it isn't the kitchen.'

'Where?' I asked, although I knew exactly what he was going to say.

'The bedroom.'

'Perhaps you could teach me,' I said.

He stopped kneading the dough and glanced at me. 'Teach you what?' he asked, unsure of my meaning.

I nodded towards the table. 'What you're doing.'

He grinned, shaking his head. 'It takes years and years of training and practice. Jerry's only just beginning to learn. How are you two getting on, by the way? I hear he took you out the other evening.'

The man was probing to discover just how far Jerry and I had gone, but we hadn't even kissed yet. It was nothing to do with Edward, although it was only natural that he should be curious.

'Yes,' I replied, 'he did.' That was all I was prepared to say. Anything else was between Jerry and me.

'I want the best for my boy,' Edward told me. 'I've had a good life in catering, and I think he will, too. Anything you can do for him . . . well, I'd appreciate it.'

I knew what he meant. He guessed that his son was still a virgin and he had good reason to suspect that I wasn't. But I pretended I didn't know what he was talking about, and I put on a puzzled expression.

'What do you mean?'

'Well . . . it's like sharing your interests. If you know something that Jerry doesn't, you could teach him.'

'Um,' I muttered. 'Like you being able to bake a

terrific cake and showing me how; that what you mean?'

Edward stared deep into my eyes, wondering if I knew more than I was letting on. 'Sort of,' he agreed. 'You want to discover the secrets which took me over two decades to learn?' He gestured towards the work-top and its various scattered ingredients.

I didn't much like cookery. At school I always seemed to make a mess of things – and unfortunately I was never able to pacify the teachers with sexual promises, because they were all women – while at home I could do just enough to survive: I could make a pot of tea, and I was able to use the toaster without burning the bread.

'Okay,' I said. 'What do I have to do?'

'First thing is to roll up your sleeves and wash your hands.'

I did as I was told. 'What is it you're making?' I asked.

Edward gestured dismissively. 'This is just some bread rolls,' he said. 'But then I'm baking a chocolate gateau with brandy, cream and fresh fruit.'

'That sounds delicious,' I said, which it did.

'There's the dough for the bread, just keep working it with your fingers,' he said. 'I'll be back in a minute.'

'I'm not very good at this,' I warned, taking hold of the lump of pastry.

'There's nothing much you can do wrong,' he assured me, then he walked out of the kitchen and left me all alone.

Little did he know, because within a few seconds the dough began sticking to the wooden surface and I had to sprinkle more flour onto it. Or at least it was my intention to sprinkle the flour, but too much poured out and it rose up like a dust cloud and went all over my blouse. I wiped at it with my hands but they were sticky with dough, and the only thing I succeeded in doing was making a mess of my top. Today was one of the days when I was wearing a bra, so I stripped off the blouse and began to shake it out. That was when Edward returned.

He stared at me. 'What are you doing?' he asked in a perplexed tone.

'I got flour all over my blouse,' I told him, and I glanced down at myself. 'You don't mind, do you? You saw more of me last week. All of me, in fact.'

'I don't mind,' he agreed, staring at my breasts and the scanty white bra which tried to constrain them. 'Do it in the nude for all I care.'

I smiled. 'You do care,' I observed.

He grinned and nodded. 'I suppose I do. All right, less of this. I'm meant to be working.' He came to stand by my side, picking up the dough and moving it nearer to me. 'You keep on with that, then divide it into twenty equal portions and roll them out so big.' He gestured with his hands.

'About the size of an erect cock?' I asked.

He looked at me, unblinking. 'It depends on the size you're used to,' he said.

'What about yours?' As I spoke, I reached behind my back and unhooked my bra, letting it drop to the floor, and my tits sprang free.

A moment later, Edward's flour-coated hands were on my breasts, stroking and rubbing them, manipulating the nipples towards their maximum dimensions.

While he fondled me, I undid the button at the top of my jeans, tugged at the zip, then thumbed the garment and my briefs down together, kicking them and my shoes aside.

Then the man's hands went around my back, dropping down to my taut buttocks and dragging me close to him. I felt the hardness of his cock against my stomach, and his mouth was against mine, his tongue forcing its way through my lips, finding my own tongue and languorously caressing it.

I slipped my hands up beneath his white jacket, surprised to find no shirt but only bare flesh, then letting my fingers slide down inside his pants and discovering that he had no underwear either. It was hot work being a chef, which is why they wore such loose clothing, and why Edward dispensed with anything under his outfit – and it made it much easier and quicker for me to strip away his clothes until he was also naked.

He lifted me up off my feet, sitting me on the table, my cunt just over the edge so that he could slip two exploring fingers inside while he bent his head to suck at my nipples. His cock was out of reach of my twat and my hands, and all I could do was run my fingers through the thick black hairs of his head as he expertly spiralled me towards the heights.

A finger on the clit is fine in its way, but I could do that for myself. What I wanted was his thick prick inside me. I'd only managed to brush my hands briefly across Edward's tool, he seemed to be deliberately keeping it away from me. I began sliding myself closer to the corner of the table, feeling the flour beneath my bottom; I planned to lower myself onto his vertical member. I had to have him inside me, and soon. We could fuck standing up, it wouldn't take long for him to bring me off.

But Edward realized what I was doing, and he pushed me back onto the worktop, removing his fingers from my aching twat and his lips from my quivering boobs. With one arm, he swept all the bowls and dishes to one side, then raised my legs and swivelled me around until I was sitting fully on the table, sideways to him. He kissed me again, our tongues thrusting together while his head forced mine further back, back, until I was lying supine. And then his lips and hands were everywhere, sucking and licking, rubbing and stroking, exploring every inch of me – down my neck, onto the swell of my breasts, then across my ribs and the flatness of my midriff, slowly but surely making their way to the inevitable target: my throbbing cunt.

I opened my legs wide in anticipation, while my

moist vaginal lips had already parted. I lay back in helpless abandon. There was no way I could get to Edward's cock before he was ready. His fingertips once again found my clitoris, touching it lightly, then withdrawing; and as I felt his hot breath against my inner labia, I closed my eyes. My whole body was writhing, my arms stretched above my head, my hips pressed up towards the man's face so that my twat could welcome his tongue a moment sooner. And still Edward teased me, drawing back and retreating when he was almost there. If he wasn't quick, I'd come before he'd even kissed my cunt.

At last I felt him make contact again, sensed something sliding in through the slippery walls of my vulva – but it was neither his tongue nor a finger, but instead something cold . . .

Whatever it was, it made my whole body ripple with sensual pleasure. I opened my eyes, raising my head slightly to see what was happening. Edward was standing by my side, casually stuffing slices of peach into my throbbing twat!

Stretched out on the table, coated with flour, I felt like some exotic creation of the master chef's.

I gasped as I realized what he was doing, watching while he lifted another piece of fruit from the bowl on the table and shoved it in. My cunt was filling up, the slivers of peach squelching against the lining of my vagina, taking up more room than even the largest of cocks.

He noticed me watching, and he licked at the peach juice which was running down his fingers, then selected another slice and began to rub it across my itching clit.

I climaxed immediately, my hips jerking up in an uncontrollable spasm, my whole body becoming locked rigid as the fantastic orgasm overwhelmed me. I gasped for air, moaning, my fingers clenching and unclenching, my heart beating frantically against the prison of my ribcage.

Before the shuddering pulses had properly died away, I felt another unique sensation in my loins and I realized that Edward was now sucking out the squashed-up peaches, swallowing down the pulpy fruit which was saturated with juice from my splendid climax.

Having the fruit drawn out of me, Edward's lips against my labia, his tongue lapping at my clitoris, was every bit as wonderful as it had been when he'd slid the fruit cocktail into my twat. Within seconds, I peaked again, and this time it was as though I'd been shot into orbit, taken to the ultimate height so swiftly that all I could do was collapse weakly onto the table. All my bones seemed to have dissolved, and I was too shattered to more than whimper my ecstatic appreciation.

I lay motionless for aeons, finally managing to focus my eyes and see Edward licking at the last drops of liquid which bubbled from his lips, a mixture of peach and cunt juice. As my pulse slowed and my breathing returned to normal, I forced myself to move. I could have lain motionless in languid luxury forever, but I still hadn't had the man's prick. He had given me everything but so far taken nothing in return.

Defeating my lethargy, I rolled onto my side, my hand reaching down and at last winning its trophy. I grasped Edward's phallus in my left hand, pulling at it, drawing him closer to me. He held back at first, and so I took a firmer hold; I wasn't gentle, because I wanted to make sure that he couldn't escape me. It was as if his ejaculation was more my priority than his, that he'd been content to make me come and wasn't interested in his own climax. To keep a proper balance, I turned over onto my front, my right hand braced to steady myself, all the time tugging the elusive cock towards my mouth. My lips parted, my tongue stretching out.

Edward was playing a game, I realized, pretending to be reluctant when in reality he was very eager. But two could play at that, and when his swollen purple glans was only a fraction of an inch from the tip of my probing tongue, I drew my head away, although I was careful to maintain a hold on his tool. I looked around, seeing the bowl full of melted chocolate which had cooled by now, and I plunged my right hand inside, bringing out a fistful of dripping liquid. I licked hungrily at my hand, rubbing it across my mouth, the melted chocolate pouring down my chin. My hand dived into the coalescing mixture again, but this time I wiped the thick dark liquid all over my other hand and Edward's captive cock.

Only then did I dip my head to lick the chocolate off his prick. The man's hips thrust forward, urging me to take his fulness into my mouth, but I contented myself with lapping at the length of his shaft, sucking the chocolate from the glans and licking off the drops which had dripped down towards his balls.

Edward's hands went to the back of my head, his fingers running through my hair and sliding across to caress my face. Soon I'd swallowed most of the chocolate which had coated his cock, and then one of his hands was suddenly in front of me, thick with more sweet dark liquid which he smeared over the end of his knob and across my face. I slurped and sucked, guzzled and gobbled.

I'd rolled onto my side again, one arm going around the man's buttocks to hold his cock close to my face. He caressed my breasts, leaving great chocolate handprints on my flesh. My pubic hairs had already become white with dustings of flour; it was as though I'd been transformed into a blonde.

The next I knew, Edward was climbing on top of the table, his cock pulling away from me as he rose, then moving back towards my mouth when he lay by my side, his own face towards my cunt. All the chocolate was gone, and for the first time I sucked his prick properly between my lips, drawing it in as far as I was able.

Edward's hands parted my thighs, twisting my hips so that my buttocks were flat on the surface. My cunt became soaking wet as he slapped a mound of melted chocolate over the lips of my labia, followed by a thick dollop of whipping cream. Next he slapped a handful of chopped fresh fruit across my groin, squashing the pulpy mixture into my twat with his fingers. Only then did his mouth descend towards the heart of my being, literally eating me out.

I could feel a slight tremor deep within me which foretold the beginnings of another orgasm; yet my exponentially increasing pleasure was heightened as I savoured Edward's cock. Licking and sucking, I was determined to give as good as I got. I sensed the knob begin to tremble, realizing that its climax was imminent, and I drew it out slightly so that my tongue could caress the purple dome of the detonator, priming it for ultimate explosion. My lips circled the ridge behind the swollen glans, but Edward suddenly drew his shaft away, grasping it in one hand. That was bad enough, but what was worse was that simultaneously he removed his tongue from my cunt.

All I could do was watch as his cock began to spurt, jetting a creamy gush of spunk down over my breasts and onto my stomach. But as it splashed warmly onto my flesh, it triggered off my own climax; my whole body shuddered and I cried out in total rapture. I grabbed hold of Edward's torso, tugging him against me, rubbing his body over mine, rolling him right across me and then down onto my other side.

Then I began to lick him all over, starting with his cock and the last drops of semen which clung to its tip, my tongue slowly moving up to his stomach and chest, tasting the heady mixture of chocolate and cream and sweat and spunk. At last we sat up, facing each other, our bodies smeared with come and all manner of other delicious ingredients. Edward reached down and wiped his hand across my twat, slipping his fingers inside and producing a handful of squashed peach and apple, banana and pear, pineapple and orange, all sodden with cunt juice. He tipped the fruit into his mouth, licking at the drips which ran down his palms. I kissed him, forcing my tongue between his lips and sucking out as much of the unique blend as he would allow me.

Edward had concocted the most sensationally hedonistic feast I'd ever tasted in my life, and we washed it down with brandy, taking it in turns to tilt the neck of the bottle between one another's lips – then swallowing the fiery liquid from the other's mouth.

A few minutes later, the man's cock was at last thrust deep within my cunt, and we fucked and fucked and fucked.

Chapter Eight

After being expelled from school, I took a full time job at Edward's restaurant. Kathy had left a couple of weeks before, and her replacement proved to be useless, so it worked out pretty well. The trouble was that I hated the work. It had been okay on Saturdays, but that was all. In fact if I could have worked just one day a week and earned enough to live on, I'd have been happy.

I wasn't cut out for waitressing, or any other job. I disliked having to spend so much time doing something I hated. But I had no qualifications, no skills, so it looked as though I'd be stuck at the restaurant until a better opportunity came along – not that I could guess what it might be.

The job had its compensations. There was Edward and his cock for a start; although I soon discovered that Helen and Petra were also claiming their share of the boss's spunk. But there were plenty of other available men to be picked up amongst the customers if ever I was in need of a fuck.

And I still had Jerry. He'd been making slow but steady progress in his exploration of my body. His kisses had become more passionate and much longer, and he'd dared to slip his hand up my thigh and touch the edge of my panties – I was always careful to wear some briefs when we were together, just in case; I didn't want to frighten him off. His major victory so far was to undo my bra from beneath my blouse, then slide his hand around to stroke my breasts and caress my nipples until they became hard. He'd even gone so far as to press his groin against my leg while we kissed, so that I could feel his rampant cock.

I was itching to see Jerry's prick, to discover if there

was any family resemblance, but I still didn't want to risk delving into his pants. He'd seemed shocked enough when I'd stroked his buttocks while we kissed, and that was through two layers of fabric. It was a mistake to have waited for so long, because in the end I lost my opportunity: Jerry walked in on his father and me while we were so busy with one another that we weren't even aware of no longer being alone.

We'd been trying out different recipes to find out which flavours we preferred mixed with spunk or cunt juice. Whenever Edward was in the kitchen, we'd always sample what he'd been making, and our method was far more exciting than simply licking it off a wooden spoon.

I was on my knees in front of the man, sucking his knob clean of the lemon icing which he'd devised for an elaborate cake that had been baked for a wedding reception to be held the following week. We were both fully dressed, his cock sticking up through his zip. Edward's back was to the door where Jerry suddenly appeared, so the boy couldn't at first see me or observe what I was doing.

The first we knew of his presence was when we heard him ask: 'Will you be needing me tomorrow?'

Tomorrow was one of my days off, and Jerry hoped to take me out into the country for the day. I'd been looking forward to it.

Edward was breathing very fast, his hips jerking, about to come. But when he heard his son's voice, he swiftly turned his head and tried to cover himself up – but too late. He took a step back, and Jerry saw me kneeling on the floor.

'What are you doing?' he asked in bewilderment, beginning to walk towards us.

I swiftly invented a story, and I was going to say how his father had spilled something and I was wiping it off his pants – but then Jerry halted, wide-eyed. And he realized that his father had indeed spilled some-thing . . . and it was dripping off my face!

I wiped at the thick drops of spunk with the back of my hand, still hoping that Jerry wouldn't recognize what it was and be too innocent to know what I'd been doing.

Jerry shook his head, staring at me, then at Edward. 'No,' he whispered. 'No! How could you?' he asked us both.

Neither of us would meet his eye, and then without another word he spun on his heel, and raced out of the door.

I looked at Edward, and I shrugged my shoulders. He nodded slowly. After he'd paid me off, I left.

There was nothing left to me in town, I decided. Mark and I had still been friends, and I'd given him a farewell to remember the night he left for university, the first time I'd ever done more than jerk him off. My first going away present was a blowjob; he'd screwed that other girl, although they'd since split up, but she'd never let him stick his tool in her mouth. One of the reasons I sucked him off was to remind myself what a cock tasted like when it wasn't covered with marzipan or fudge or meringue.

Mark would have been happy with me just licking his dick, and after he'd poured his hot come down my throat he'd claimed he was so spent that he wouldn't be able to get his prick up again for hours. I proved him wrong, and then I allowed him to drill his way into me. I had to let him know that I was better at fucking than his ex-girlfriend, and I succeeded. He had plenty of spunk in reserve, and in bringing him off I reached orgasm myself three times. Mark had taught me a lot, but I'd done much for him in return; so a goodbye fuck was the last I could offer.

Although we'd been seeing less and less of each other until then, I missed Mark once he'd gone and I envied the way he'd been able to escape. I wished I'd had his brains, but perhaps I could get by without.

It was time for me to head to the city.

There was no point paying for the journey. I didn't

have that much saved, and I'd need it for when I arrived. All I had to do was hitch a ride. Being a girl on my own, I guessed that I wouldn't have too much trouble finding a lift.

I'd never hitch-hiked before, and as I stood by the side of the highway, my one bag of belongings at my feet, I stuck out my thumb for the first time at the line of cars and vans and trucks which thundered by.

A car stopped within a few minutes, gliding to a halt ten yards beyond me. A couple of seconds later, as I was picking up my bag to go to the first vehicle, another one skidded to a screeching halt by my side. I didn't know much about cars, but the second one was bigger, shinier, newer. It was an easy choice, and so I pulled at the door handle and ducked my head to climb inside. Then I noticed the driver.

It was a woman, and for some reason that surprised me. But I slid onto the plush upholstery of the passenger seat, turning my head towards her.

'Thanks,' I said.

'No trouble,' she replied, staring at me. 'Don't I know you? You look familiar.'

If a guy had said that, I'd have thought it was a clichéd pickup line. But I didn't recognize the woman, so I shook my head. 'I don't think so.'

She shrugged. 'Maybe I'm wrong.' Glancing in the mirror, she floored the accelerator and the car shot off. 'Where you heading?'

I nodded down the road. 'To the city.'

'It's your lucky day,' the driver told me. 'I'm going all the way.' Her eyes still on the road, she tapped her bag which was on the edge of the seat next to me. 'Do you want a cigarette?'

'No thanks,' I told her. Smoking was a phase I'd been through with Mark, but unlike masturbation it hadn't caught on.

'Light me one,' she said, and it was more of an order than a request.

I opened her bag and found the pack of cigarettes, pulling one out and offering it to her.

'I can't,' she told me, with a swift shake of her head, 'not when I'm driving. You light it for me.'

Sticking the filtertip in my mouth, I put the lighter to the other end of the cigarette, inhaled to make sure it was lit properly, then passed it to the woman. She turned her mouth to me, and I slid the cigarette between her lips.

'Thanks,' she said, blowing twin plumes of smoke from her nostrils.

I noticed she was driving very fast, in the outside lane and overtaking all the other traffic. But it didn't seem as though we were speeding, rather as though all the other vehicles were going very slow. She drove confidently and easily. I automatically assumed that it was her husband's car, or that he'd bought it for her, but there was no wedding ring on her finger.

She was in her late thirties, I guessed, with cropped red hair, although the colour seemed far too bright to be natural; she wore pale lipstick and very subtle makeup, and her face was thin with sharp angular features. She was slim, wearing a well-cut and expensive dark blue woollen trouser suit and what looked like a man's shirt and a tie; but the shirt was of black satin, the tie pure white silk.

'Had you been waiting there long?' she asked.

'No, a few minutes.'

'That's what I suspected. A pretty girl like you shouldn't have had much trouble getting a lift. You're lucky I happened along.'

'Because you're heading to the city?' I asked.

'Partly that. But the odds are you'd have been picked up by a man, and it's always risky for a girl getting a lift from a male – particularly dressed the way you are.' Her eyes took in my outfit: the knee-length white leather boots with the criss-cross laces, the short black velvet skirt, the tight crimson sweater which emphasized the outline of my breasts rather than concealed them.

I shrugged, not answering. One of the reasons I'd dressed in such a way was to make it easier for me to find a lift. And I'd also liked the idea of being picked up by a man. Preferably a big muscular hunk of a truck driver, because who could tell what it might lead to . . . ?

'Yes, I suppose it was lucky,' I agreed. 'It seems you're the person who'll get me to the city quickest.'

'I love driving fast,' the woman said. 'And men so hate it when they're overtaken by a mere female. But there's very little on the road which can beat this beauty.' She ran her fingers lightly across the rim of the steering wheel.

'It's a nice car,' I said. 'Is it yours?'

'Of course it's mine,' she answered, turning her head to gaze at me. 'Who's did you think it was?'

I thought fast. 'The company you work for,' I said.

The woman nodded, just once. 'Yes, you're half right. It is a company car, but as it's my company . . .'

She sounded very proud, so I tried to look impressed. 'What sort of company?'

'We import herbs and spices, sell them through health stores and delicatessens.'

'Do you supply restaurants?' I asked.

'That's right.'

I asked her if she knew Edward's place, and she said she called on him every month.

'That's where I saw you!' she added. 'I thought I knew you from somewhere; I never forget a pretty girl. My name's Vera, by the way.'

I couldn't remember having seen her, but that wasn't really surprising. Edward always dealt with business from his office, the restaurant had hundreds of custom-ers a week – and it was only the men that I ever really noticed.

I'd felt a little tense since entering the car, but now I began to relax and we talked more easily. Vera asked where I was heading for in the city, whether I had any friends there, a job lined up, a place to stay. I told her that I intended to stay in a cheap hotel at first, then look for work and a place of my own.

'You don't have to do that,' Vera said. 'I've got a huge apartment right in the centre of the city. If you like, you can stay in one of the spare rooms until you're settled.'

'That's very kind of you,' I said, 'but I couldn't possibly accept.'

'It's up to you. But don't think I'm doing it out of the goodness of my heart. I'm not there that often, and what I need is someone to take care of the place while I'm away. I did have someone until recently, but she . . . she left. If you did agree to stay, you'd be doing me a favour.'

'Really?' I asked doubtfully.

'Yes, really. Tell you what: It'll be late when we arrive, you won't want to go searching for somewhere to stay. Why don't you spend the night at my place? Give it a try. Then if you want to find somewhere tomorrow, fine. But you've got nothing to lose, have you?'

'No, I suppose not.' I considered the idea for a few seconds, realizing that it would be a lot easier if I did as the woman suggested. 'Okay,' I agreed. 'Thanks.'

'Good, good.'

We drove on down the highway, the powerful car eating up the miles.

The vehicle had slowed as it entered the city and the queues of traffic, and I stared out of the window, at the wide streets and the tall buildings.

'Why don't we have something to eat first?' Vera suggested. 'You must be hungry. I know I am.'

I turned to look at her. 'Yes, I suppose I am.'

'Fine. There's a terrific Malaysian restaurant I know,

very expensive but very good. Do you like Malaysian food?'

I didn't know, I'd never tried it, but I probably would; there was very little I didn't like. But a very expensive restaurant . . . ?

Vera must have guessed what I was thinking, because she said, 'If it's the money you're bothered about, don't. The company's paying. It's all down to expenses. If I claim that you're an important client, taking you out to dinner will reduce our tax liability a little.' She glanced at me. 'I hate dining alone, so if you don't come with me that means we'll both go hungry. And what's the point of that?'

'All right,' I said. If she could afford it, and she clearly could, I wasn't averse to helping her spend her money.

We parked the car a few minutes later, then walked around the corner to the restaurant. The place was furnished in bamboo, with cane chairs and tables, and there were palm trees in the corners and rubber plants everywhere, creeping up most of the walls.

Vera was evidently a regular patron, because the head waiter welcomed her like an old friend, taking her coat, offering her the menu as we sat down at a low table in the bar, asking if she'd have her usual aperitif. I felt out of place here, thinking that I wasn't dressed smartly enough; probably I half believed that I ought not to have been here at all, not as a client, that really I should have been serving at the tables.

I chose the same drink as Vera, because I couldn't think of any other, a martini. She pointed out some of the highlights on the menu – none of it was written in English.

'Why don't you just order what you think I'll like?' I suggested. 'It'll make things simpler.'

'Good idea,' she said, clearly preferring to choose for me. 'Let me see . . .'

Finally we went through into the dining room. The meal consisted of several small dishes placed on trays

99

warmed by candles, all of which were served at once and to which we helped ourselves. I had to admit it was all very delicious, and I was full before I'd eaten my share. Vera ordered a bottle of wine. I wasn't used to alcohol, and I drank it like a soft drink, but she kept on refilling my glass.

'Did you leave your boyfriend behind?' she asked.

We'd been talking throughout the meal, but about nothing in particular, and her question seemed out of context and took me by surprise. I shook my head quickly, too quickly.

'What happened?' asked Vera.

I didn't answer, not sure what to say. Jerry had been my boyfriend, technically.

'Did you have a row? Is that why you wanted to get away from town?' She was being very casual in her questioning, not looking at me and pretending that it didn't matter whether I answered; but she was clearly interested in what I might say.

Jerry and I hadn't had an argument, not as such. I hadn't seen him since the incident when he'd caught me with his father's cock in my mouth and the man's come all over my face.

I shrugged. 'I didn't have a boyfriend, not really.'

Vera raised one eyebrow, doubtfully. 'Males can be such beasts, can't they?' Her hand reached out to rest on mine; I was about to draw my hand away, but for some reason I didn't. 'I can imagine what you've been through.'

I simply looked at the woman, narrowing my eyelids to see her properly; for some reason I was having trouble focusing. She was wrong, I thought. She could have no idea, couldn't possibly imagine what I'd been through.

'Whatever's happened to you,' she continued, 'I can feel for you, because the same has happened to me. What did he do, this boy of yours?'

I half smiled, because that was the problem. Jerry hadn't done anything. If he had, or if I'd encouraged him more, then perhaps I wouldn't have needed his father. Perhaps, though unlikely. Jerry was just a boy, Edward a man – and even Edward hadn't been sufficient for me at times.

Vera's hand was gently stroking mine. She leaned over the table between us, lowering her voice so that she couldn't be overheard. 'Did he try to touch you? Did he? Did you let him? You should never let them touch you.'

I shook my head, reaching for my wine and taking a mouthful. 'No, he didn't touch me. Not really.'

'Not really? What does that mean?'

I shrugged.

'Did he touch your legs?' Vera persisted. 'You've got nice legs, long and shapely. What about your breasts? They give you a nice profile. He must have tried to touch them. Did he slip his hand inside your sweater? Did he touch your flesh, did he?'

I stared at Vera. I could hear her questions quite clearly, but they didn't seem to make sense; they had nothing to do with me. This was some nightmare interrogation, like the ones when I dreamed I was back at school and being asked the most stupid questions.

'All that's only the preliminary, you know,' Vera continued, gazing deep into my eyes. 'They don't really want your legs or your breasts, what they really want to touch is your pussy. You must have a lovely pussy, all soft and smooth. And it isn't just their hands they want to touch you with. They'll try and stick their ugly thing inside you. That's all they want. And once they've stuck it in you and left a horrible sticky mess inside your body, they'll just go and leave you. They're all like that.' She shook her head angrily. 'Males!' she spat the word out then pulled a face, as though it had left a nasty taste in her mouth.

Reaching for my glass, I put it to my mouth again; but it was empty. I shook my head in denial. Vera was wrong, men weren't all like that. And not Jerry, he'd

101

never touched me – not touched me in the way she meant . . . and the way I'd wanted.

'He never touched me,' I assured her, meeting her gaze. For some reason it was vitally important that I could make her believe this.

'Are you sure?' she asked doubtfully. 'He didn't touch your pussy, try to put his hand on it, slip his finger inside?'

'No.'

'What about his thing? He must have pulled that out and shown it to you, all big and hard and ugly. Did he?'

'No.'

'He must have done,' Vera said. 'Didn't he make you touch it, ask you to stroke it, to rub it, to squeeze all the evil fluid from it?'

'He didn't, he didn't, he didn't.' I shook my head vigorously.

Vera let go of my hand and leaned back in her seat. She turned her head, watching me from the corners of her eyes.

'If he didn't do any of that,' she asked, 'why did you have a row and leave town?'

I sighed. 'But we didn't have a row.' I picked up my glass again; it was still empty. 'Can I have some more wine?'

'I think you've had enough,' Vera told me.

Resting my right elbow on the table, and my chin in the palm of my hand, I stared at the woman. 'What's going on?' I asked slowly, carefully enunciating my words so as not to slur them. 'What are all these questions about?'

'I have to be sure,' she answered mysteriously, 'that's all.'

'Sure of what?' I wanted to know.

Vera twisted the stem of her wine glass between her fingers, even her eyes no longer looking directly at me. 'You remind me so much of myself when I was your age, or perhaps a little older. I just wondered if you'd had to put up with the same kind of things that I did before I knew better.'

'Knew better?' I repeated. 'What do you mean?'

'It doesn't matter,' she said, but after all her questioning I knew that the opposite was true: it mattered a lot, although I'd no idea why. 'Are you ready to leave? I'll call the waiter.'

She paid by credit card, leaving a big tip, then we left the restaurant. The cool evening breeze was welcome after the heat inside, and I took a deep breath; but as we began to walk to Vera's car, I felt dizzy.

'Are you okay?' the woman asked, reaching out to support me as I staggered and almost slipped over.

Everything around me began to spin, and I leaned back against the wall of the building we were passing, but even the wall was moving, the ground beneath me tilting.

'Come on,' I heard Vera say, her voice echoing within my skull. 'Come on, come on, come on . . .'

Her arm went around my shoulder, urging me to keep moving.

'We're nearly at the car,' she said. 'At the car, at the car, at the car . . .'

We reached the vehicle, and the woman opened the passenger door and helped me inside, unwinding the window, then hurrying around to the other door.

'If you're going to be sick,' she told me. 'Be sick, be sick, be sick . . . Then try and do it out of the window. Of the window, of the window, of the window . . .'

But I didn't feel nauseous, I simply felt totally weak, that I had no control over my limbs; I was a prisoner within my own body. Vera started the car, and I stared out of the window, watching all the lights of the other vehicles flash by – the brilliant white of dazzling headlamps, the flaring red of tail-lights, the on-off winking orange of indicators; and these were mixed up with the illumination from the side of the road – the glare of shop windows, the flashing neon of advertisements, the red and amber and green patterns

103

of traffic lights. It was like something from a science fiction movie; a vision of the future, all fast moving and garishly coloured.

I can hardly remember arriving at Vera's place. When we were inside, only isolated fragments of memory remained: the explosion of sound as the woman slammed the car door; stumbling up a row of steps and waiting while a key was thrust into the wide door; seeing two people zig-zagging towards us, a woman and a girl who seemed about to fall over, then realizing that I was watching my own image in a huge mirror by the side of the elevator.

Then somehow I was inside a room and sitting on the edge of a bed, Vera kneeling in front of me and unfastening the laces of my boots, tugging them off my feet and then reaching for the buttons on the waistband of my skirt.

'I can do that,' I told her, knocking her hand away and fumbling with the buttons, at last succeeding in undoing them, rising steadily to my feet and allowing the skirt to drop to the floor. Then I started tugging off my sweater, managing to get it up over my face, but with my vision blocked I couldn't fix my bearings and I slipped, falling back onto the bed.

I felt Vera helping me, pulling the garment off me, and then I could see again. She was gazing down at me. I wore only my black underwear, the lacy bra and the matching brief panties, and I felt strangely vulnerable. I scrabbled at the bed covers, trying to slide beneath them and into safety.

Vera's hand reached out towards me, and I moved aside, but she was only helping me with the bed clothes. I rolled between the cold sheets, snuggling down, my head sinking into the soft pillow while Vera tucked the covers up under my chin.

'Goodnight,' she whispered, then she leaned across and lightly kissed my forehead.

The light went out, and I was alone and asleep within seconds.

Chapter Nine

The next morning, I felt different. Not better, just different. I could stand up straight without too much trouble, but my head was throbbing and my mouth and throat were very dry.

I stared around the room where I'd slept, aware of it for the first time, noticing the soft pastel colours of the walls and ceiling, the expensive furnishings. It was a very feminine room, that was the only way I could describe it, very soft and gentle. I simply had to have a drink of water and so I opened the door, searching for the kitchen, and I found myself in a long corridor. There were a number of doors on either side of the passage, and I tried them all in turn, finding the bathroom, lounge, and then Vera's bedroom.

The woman was fast asleep, curled up in the centre of a huge bed. I stared at the bed, because I'd never seen anything like it. It was circular, and like most of the furnishings in the room it was black – black covers, black pillows. The walls were black, so were the window frames and the curtains, the fitted wardrobes, the dressing table in a corner alcove, the two chests of drawers, and also a huge metal padlocked trunk by the side of the bed. Even the ceiling seemed to be black, but that was because it reflected the colour of the rest of the room; the ceiling was completely covered in hexagonal mirrors, which fitted together like a huge mosaic.

The only splashes of colour in the room were the pictures which hung across the wall opposite the bed. They were like the pin-ups in a boy's bedroom. But these weren't simply posters or illustrations torn from a magazine; they were framed, some of them photographs, the rest paintings or drawings. There must have been a dozen of them in all: Girls on their own or with another girl, either naked or scantily clad; one girl touching the naked breast of another, two girls kissing. The one which caught my eye was a line drawing of two voluptuous nudes lying side by side, each with a hand between the other's legs.

One of the other walls was also decorated, but in a different and oddly disturbing style. It was hung with old weapons and hunting trophies – a long-barrelled musket, a pair of flintlock pistols, a battered hide shield, a curved Japanese sword, a pair of crossed African spears, even a harpoon; a single ivory tusk, the stuffed head of a growling lion, a stretched out tiger skin, a pair of buffalo horns mounted on a plaque. I didn't doubt that all of the guns and blades were genuine antiques; and the gruesome trophies also belonged to another generation.

The naked girls, the weapons, the dead animals – it hardly seemed like the bedroom of a woman. But in the midst of all this, Vera slept peacefully on. I closed the door again, continuing my quest for the oasis of the kitchen.

Finally I found it, an immaculately gleaming room crammed full of every labour saving culinary device I'd ever heard of or could imagine. After a brief search, I located the cups and turned on the cold tap above the sink, drinking what must have been at least a pint of water. I wondered about making Vera a cup of tea or coffee, but decided it might be best to let her sleep on. What I needed was an aspirin, but given enough time my headache would go away; I could manage without.

I decided to take a shower, maybe that would wash the cobwebs away and make me feel better; I was certain Vera wouldn't mind – all I needed was her hot water, I had my own soap and sponge and towel. Returning to the bedroom where I'd slept, I peeled off my undies and then headed for the bathroom. Once under the shower, I allowed the needle sharp spray of hot water to splash luxuriously all over me. While I was there, I took the opportunity to wash my hair as well. I left the shower reluctantly. The water was so lovely and relaxing, I could have stayed beneath it for hours.

I was drying myself when I noticed the door handle turn.

'Just a moment,' I called, and I quickly wrapped the towel around myself before opening the door. If it had been a man outside, it wouldn't have bothered me for him to see me in the nude; but it was somehow different for a woman. I opened the door.

'Hi,' said Vera. 'Feeling better this morning?'

'Yes, thanks,' I replied. 'I've just had a shower, I hope it was all right. But I've finished if you want to come in.'

She shook her head, making no attempt to enter the bathroom. 'No, I was only checking to see if you were okay.'

Her eyes surveyed my body. The towel covered me from the top of my breasts to halfway down my thighs. Vera was wearing a pair of pyjamas, big and loose-fitting like a man's.

'Your skin's a little dry,' she said. 'I've got some cream in the cabinet there, why don't you rub some in? I'll go and make a pot of coffee. You want some?'

'Please,' I replied, and then she turned away. I pushed the door shut, removed the towel and contin-ued drying myself. When I'd finished I opened the cabinet on the wall above the basin and searched through the bottles and boxes of shampoo, deodorant, talc, perfume, bath oils and lotions, until I came across the plastic tube of cream which I assumed Vera meant. I squeezed a blob of it onto the back of my left hand, then rubbed it in with the tips of my right hand fingers. It was very thick, but my skin absorbed it in no time. I began massaging it into my arms.

Then I sensed the door opening behind me. I glanced over my shoulder as Vera stepped inside the room. If I'd pushed open a door and seen someone naked inside, someone of the same sex, I'd quickly have retreated. But Vera didn't, and her eyes explored my bare back and bottom and thighs.

It would have seemed foolish to hurriedly cover myself up, so I carried on spreading the cream into my left arm, waiting for her to leave. But instead she came closer.

'Let me help you,' she said. 'I'll do your back.' She took the tube from me and squeezed some cream onto her hand, then began rubbing it into my back.

It felt cold for a moment, but she worked it into my supple flesh with a circular movement, all across my shoulder blades then down my spine. Her touch sent a shiver rippling across my body, a very pleasant shiver. Her hand reached my waist and then began to move across the flare of my buttocks, but then she was out of cream and had to squeeze some more into her palm. I heard her rub both of her hands together. She didn't carry on where she'd reached, instead her hands stroked at my shoulders before sliding down my sides, slipping beneath my arms and inching towards my front.

My nipples were already erect by the time her fingers brushed against the curves of my breasts. Her hands continued to glide further and further over my flesh until her palms cupped my boobs, gently stroking them. I stayed quite still. I should have pushed her away as soon as I realized what she was planning, but by now it was too late – and the reason I hadn't tried to escape was because I liked it, it felt so good to have a pair of hands caressing my body, any hands.

Then her right hand began to move downwards, down, down, until its fingertips became entangled in my pubic hairs. Vera pressed against my pelvic bone, rubbing and rubbing and rubbing. Her head nuzzled against the back of my neck, her tongue darting out to lick the tender skin behind my left ear. I leaned my head back, turning it, my lips met hers, and we kissed.

It didn't matter that she was a woman. She had lips

and a tongue, and that was all that was needed. Our lips rubbed together, our tongues duelling hard, and her hands were still at work on my breast and pubis. She squeezed my left nipple between her fingers as her hand circled my breast, while the heel of her other hand ground against my crotch. I spread my legs a little, hoping that maybe she would divert an exploratory finger into my moist cunt; but she refused the invitation.

I was unable to reach her with my own hands, yet I didn't want to turn to face her because that would have meant she'd have had to stop the wonderful things she was doing to my body.

At last Vera pulled her mouth from mine. 'Let's go into my room,' she said, withdrawing her hands from me. She turned and walked out of the bathroom, along the corridor and into her bedroom.

As I followed her, I felt both nervous and exhilarated, unsure of exactly what was to come but eagerly anticipating the experience. There was no doubt in my mind that I was going to have sex with Vera, about to try lesbianism for the first time.

Entering her room, I glanced around as though I hadn't seen it before. The curtains were still closed, but enough light filtered through them. The room only took my interest for a second, because the woman was the main focus of my attention. She closed the door behind me, then gestured towards the unusual bed. Obediently, I went across and lay down, my feet towards her. I knew how keen men were on seeing the secret zone which lay between my thighs, and so I opened my legs. It might have been different for Vera, because her cunt couldn't have been that dissimilar to mine, but it seemed the right thing to do.

For a second I stared up at myself in the ceiling mirrors, watching my nude body, admiring it as though it were another person.

The woman walked slowly towards me, expressionless, and she sat on the edge of the bed, turning to face me. She gazed at my nude supine body, from the tips of my toes to the crown of my head, but paying particular attention to both my gaping twat and my breasts. I wanted to see her body, and I was tempted to reach out and unfasten the buttons of her pyjama jacket; but I decided I ought to let her lead the way. In this kind of situation, I was a mere novice.

'You're gorgeous,' Vera breathed. 'You really are. Your body's been designed for loving.'

She climbed onto the bed by my side, and I rolled over to face her. Propping herself up on her left elbow, her right hand glided across my flesh, stroking my face, caressing my breasts, rubbing the curve of my left hip, fingering my pubic curls. Her touch was electric, stimulating every nerve ending; and I wanted to do the same to her, but instead I simply let her do what she wished with me.

Her mouth moved against mine, and we kissed again, hard and passionately. Our lips squashed together, our teeth clashed, our tongues fought for domination. Vera's fingers were still tentatively exploring the fringes of my cunt, and I ached for them inside me. A woman must have sensed another woman's sexual desires far more than any man. Vera would know how to stroke her own cunt, and I waited and wished for her to share her knowledge with my own itching twat.

And it was true, she knew exactly what I wanted and needed. She drew her face away, gazing down at her fingers and my cunt.

'Is pussy hungry?' she asked. 'Does pussy want something to eat?'

As she spoke, a fingertip gently eased its way between my inner labia and lightly touched my clitoris. I thrust my hips forward in pleasure, but then the finger was sliding out again.

'If pussy behaves herself,' Vera added, 'then pussy will get more than enough.' She caressed the soft hairs of my cunt, just as if she was stroking a pet animal.

110

'I want it now,' I said, speaking for the first time since Vera had returned to the bathroom.

'Who wants it now?' she asked.

'Pussy,' I told her. 'Pussy wants it now.'

'Pussy must learn to wait,' Vera told me. 'The more pussy waits, the hungrier she'll be and the more she'll appreciate it when she's given something to eat.' Her fingertips tapped against my pubic bone, as if lightly chastising me.

Her hand went to my shoulder, roughly pushing me on my back, and suddenly she was kneeling above me, her legs on either side of my hips. She seized my arms at the wrists, raising them above my head and pinning them down, transferring her grip so that she could hold me with a single hand. I tried to get free, to see if I was able, but Vera was much stronger than she looked.

With her free hand she rubbed at my breasts, no longer so gently, but not too roughly. She inched her way further down the bed, until she was straddling my hips, and her head bent towards me. I parted my lips, waiting for her kiss, but instead her mouth descended to my right breast, the tongue ringing the dimpled aureola, around and around, the sensation driving me wild and causing my whole body to writhe and wriggle; then she transferred her attentions to my left nipple, sucking and sucking until it throbbed, while her hand manipulated my right boob.

My arms were still trapped as Vera stretched out on top of me, and instinctively I spread my legs wide, as I would have done for a man. Her legs slipped between my thighs, and she began to stroke her crotch against mine, rubbing hard on top of me, almost exactly as if she'd had a cock inside my cunt and was fucking me – and it felt nearly as good. I responded with equal ardour, thrusting my pubis at hers and grinding it against her pelvic bone.

Her free hand roved expertly across my flesh, know-ing precisely which parts of my body were the most sensitive to her touch, and her lips pressed against mine as we kissed harder than ever, breathing the same air, our heartbeats synchronized.

My breath came faster and faster, my hips jerking harder and harder, and then I climaxed in a shuddering crescendo of ecstasy.

Vera let go of my hands and she levered herself up, staring analytically at my face. My whole body was damp with sweat, but she seemed cool and composed. I realized that she couldn't have had an orgasm, and I felt totally selfish. I reached up, grasping the top button of her pyjama jacket, but she slapped my hand away and climbed off me.

'The coffee must be ready,' she announced. 'How do you like it? Black or white? Sugar?'

I watched as she strode to the door. 'Black, please,' I said, surprised. 'One sugar.'

Then she was gone, and I was left on my own on the bed. As my pulse slowed and I regained my breath, I reached down between my legs, feeling the dampness from my climax dripping from my twat. I'd enjoyed it, but there seemed something missing. Perhaps it was because I'd taken everything and given nothing in return, and I wasn't used to that.

Vera returned a couple of minutes later, holding a silver tray with two bone china cups and saucers. I sat up and she handed me one of the cups, then she climbed onto the bed next to me, crossing her legs. We drank our coffee in silence.

There was so much I wanted to say and to ask, but I didn't know where to begin; and I also wondered whether any of it was worth saying or asking. When in doubt, do nothing, and things will always eventually sort themselves out.

'What do you want to do today?' Vera finally asked, once her cup was empty.

I shrugged a reply.

'You said you were after a job and somewhere to live,' she reminded me.

112

'I'm in no hurry if you're not,' I told her.

The woman nodded, and slowly she smiled. 'I think we're going to get on very well together, you and I.'

In all the time we spent together, I don't think Vera ever had a climax. She enjoyed what we did – or rather what she did to me – but she would never let me reciprocate. I was never allowed to touch her cunt, and I only ever saw her pink vaginal folds by chance. She didn't even like me to stroke her breasts. Kissing was the only sexual contact I was allowed to make. She would never talk about any of this. They were her rules, and it was up to me to abide by them.

Yet I so often wondered what her twat tasted like, how it felt to run my tongue through her cunt lips and suck at her clitoris.

She did that to me often enough, and it was terrific, she was a real expert. Why she didn't wish to share such pleasure was a mystery to me, but after a time I came to accept it. Her satisfaction seemed to derive from controlling me, of making me come.

Vera provided everything for me. I shared her home, but although we were lovers I had my own room. Sometimes she would summon me to her bedroom, other times she would come to me; if I dared to make the first move, I would be spurned and rejected and have to provide my own orgasm in my lonely bed. Vera paid for my clothes and food, she took me out to dinner and to see shows; she even gave me money of my own. All she asked was that I was available whenever she wanted. She was always the dominant partner, adopting the masculine role in our relationship, and it was as though I was her mistress.

I longed to reverse our roles just once, but it was never to be.

As well as lying on top of me, her pubic bone stroking against mine, Vera gave me orgasms with her tongue and her fingers, and even on one occasion with her toes. But her favourite method was to use a vibrator or even an artificial penis.

I'd heard of vibrators, of course, but I'd never seen any until Vera first used one on me. At first I was very wary of it. I'd never had anything like that stuck up my cunt before, but as soon as she switched it on and rubbed it against my nipples and my whole body started tingling, I wished I'd known about them before. She stroked my breasts and slid the thing down between my legs, gently massaging my thighs before slowly working up against my labia and onto my clit. I tried to grab the vibrator from her, to shove it inside me, impatient to have it right up my twat; but she was too strong for me, and as punishment withdrew it from my moist lips for a few seconds, while I begged her to slide it into me. And I came almost as soon as its trembling head made contact with my soft flesh.

Vera had quite a collection, different designs and shapes; smooth thin ones, fat knobbly ones, ones with vibrating glans-shaped heads, even ones which could ejaculate liquid deep into my cunt – warm milk as imitation semen. I often wondered if she used these on herself when I was out of the room . . . because whenever she was away, I certainly made good use of them!

One thing that I never had access to, whether Vera was away or not, was the metal trunk in her room. It was always kept padlocked, and she carried the key with her all the time. I discovered what the mysterious trunk contained the first day I stayed with her; and as soon as I found out, I wished that I'd never asked . . .

We had already spent most of the morning fucking. Vera had given me another orgasm with her fingers sliding in my cunt; and after that she had knelt on the floor, her head between my thighs, while my legs hung over the edge of the circular bed. I stared up at the ceiling, watching our reflections, but there wasn't much I could see except the back of Vera's head. I levered myself up on my elbows, hoping to observe her busy tongue lapping at my vagina, but her mouth was right up against my labia and my view was blocked.

But if I could see nothing, I could feel plenty – and the sensation was overpowering. I'd been licked out before, many times, but I soon discovered that Vera was a cunt connoisseur. From the very start she gave me better head than any man ever had. Being a woman, she had to specialize with her tongue, I guessed; not having a cock, she didn't have to divide her talents.

My fingers ruffled her red hair as her tongue thrust deeper and deeper, stroking the walls of my vagina, while her nose was pressed hard against my clit and I felt her breath against my cunt lips. And when I came, my whole body erupted in a frenzy of passion. I cried out as I reached my helpless moment of rapture, trying to stretch the brief instant into eternity.

Vera pulled her head away and stood up, her mouth wet with saliva and my orgasmic juices, her tongue flicking out to suck her lips dry.

I lay stretched out on the bed staring at her. I was still nude, I hadn't dressed all day, while Vera continued to wear her pyjamas. I'd neither seen her nor touched her properly; and whenever I tried to pull at her garments or more than kiss her, she would firmly slap me down.

'Can't I love you?' I asked.

'You are,' she replied.

'But I want to see you, to touch your body.'

'No one touches me,' Vera answered coldly. 'No one.'

I continued gazing at her, or more precisely at what she was wearing. Did she have something to hide? Was she scarred from an operation or an accident? Was her flesh somehow disfigured?

She half smiled, thinking of what I'd said about wanting to see her. 'There isn't much to see,' she said. 'You'd be disappointed.'

'That's up to me to decide.'

Vera shook her head wistfully. She backed away

until she was standing in front of the trunk, and one of her hands slid idly across its surface.

'What's in there?' I asked.

She replied with a question of her own. 'Is pussy still hungry?' she wanted to know.

I reached down and touched my cunt. I was always ready for more, particularly when it was offered to me – I'd had to do very little but lie back and accept Vera's attentions. Never had fucking been so easy or pleasurable.

In answer, I parted my inner labia and let her see into the dark pink recesses of my twat. My cunt and I were here and waiting for whatever she had to offer.

'Pussy has had the appetizer,' Vera said. 'But can she take the main course? It may be more than she can swallow.'

I said nothing, all I did was brace my legs on the floor and thrust my open crotch towards the woman.

Vera nodded, and she started to unbutton her pyjama jacket. One button, two. But before she got any further, she reached in through the top and pulled out a brass key on a silver chain, slipping the chain over her head and sliding the key into the padlock of the black metal chest. She unhinged the locked, lifted the hasp, then threw open the trunk lid.

I couldn't see inside from where I lay, not even via the mirrored ceiling. But I didn't sit up; I could wait.

'You must close your eyes,' Vera told me. 'No peeping.'

I shut my eyes.

'And pussy mustn't see, either,' said Vera, and she stepped back towards the bed, flicking the top cover over me, hiding me from face to cunt.

I waited, listening. I heard the rustle of fabric as she removed her pyjamas, and I almost risked a peep at her nude body. Then came the muted sounds of her sorting through the contents of the trunk, and I heard something jingle.

Two minutes later came her voice.

'All right,' she ordered, in a harsher voice than she'd used before, 'look at me!'

I threw the cover aside, blinking against the light, and then suddenly my eyes focused on Vera. I stared in amazement and sat up. I'd never seen or imagined anything like the sight with which I was confronted.

The woman was wearing a leather hood, a black mask which followed the contours of her face, leaving only two narrow slits for her eyes. The mask completely hid her head, except for her mouth and chin, and it was fastened beneath the jaw by a thick buckled strap.

More straps held the tight leather jerkin which she wore around her torso. This was also black and it covered her from shoulder to navel, and it was studded with shiny metal rings from which were looped links of bright silver chain. There were two holes in the leather, through which thrust the woman's bare breasts. They were small, but firm – and she'd previously painted her nipples with black lipstick.

Her arms were bare, but she wore heavy gauntlets, again of black leather. And in her right hand she carried the handle of a whip, a thick rod which grew into a vicious length of plaited leather. In her left, she carried a pair of manacles.

She was naked beneath the jerkin, except for –

– a giant phallus which jutted from her crotch, held there by straps around her waist and thighs.

But none of this looked ridiculous. Instead she was an awesome, terrifying spectacle, and I found myself drawing away from her and sliding to the edge of the bed by the wall.

'It's time to feed pussy a proper meal,' Vera announced in her strange fierce voice.

I gasped. She couldn't mean it. There was no way that my cunt could accept such a monster. The dildo was modelled from a penis, complete with the vein on the underside, the ridge behind the head, the glans itself. Like the rest of Vera's bizarre garb, it was completely black. But it was so huge, at least twelve inches long and two inches across at the base.

Vera threw the manacles towards me, and they clattered onto the bed by my side. 'Put them on!' she instructed.

I picked them up, two thick metal bracelets joined by a few inches of sturdy chain, and I obeyed; I clamped them around my wrists as though they were jewellery.

As she moved towards me, I knew she intended to fuck me, to do it for real this time. But it was impossible, there was no way my cunt could take that gargantuan thing which stood between her legs.

Yet in a weird way I was beginning to get excited as I stared at the woman, at her black-tipped breasts, even at her cunt – the base of the phallus was resting against her pelvic bone, and I could clearly see the vertical slit which led to her vagina. Vera, I observed, had shaved off all her pubic hairs.

She raised one leg and lifted herself onto the bed, standing above me, her legs apart, and I was just able to see into the pink cleft of her cunt.

The knotted tip of the whip flicked against my own twat, and I tried to creep further away, but I was up against the wall and there could be no retreat.

'Open your mouth, pussy,' Vera commanded.

As if of their own volition, my legs spread wide. Vera grabbed my feet and tugged me down onto my back and towards her. She held the whip against my throat with one hand as she knelt down between my thighs, while her other hand aimed the hard rubber end of her artificial cock at my cunt.

This time there was no kissing, no caressing, no display of affection. The tip of the phallus touched my clit, and a wave of joy rippled through me. And as Vera plunged into me, I was aware that this was pure sex, absolute animal lust – and I loved it!

I thought it might hurt, that I would be too dry, that it was too large for me; but Vera didn't ram her weapon

118

to the hilt, and her thrusts were rhythmic and sensual. It did hurt a little, but I hardly noticed. The pleasure outweighed the pain.

Vera used the phallus as though it was a part of her body, altering the speed and length of stroke as she drove into me. I needn't have worried about the ersatz prick being unlubricated, because within seconds my cunt was dripping wet from my first blissful climax.

I gazed up at the leather mask. Anyone could have been fucking me, anyone at all. And as I strived for my second orgasm, I tried to imagine who I'd have preferred to be screwing me.

Then I realized it didn't matter, it didn't matter at all.

Chapter Ten

It was very pleasant living with Vera, because I didn't have to do anything at all except fuck her. Everything was provided, I didn't even need to think; my existence was reduced to reacting.

But after a time I began to miss certain things. Things like the feel of a warm cock in my cunt, the taste of spunk in my mouth, a kiss that was rough with unshaven stubble.

There was a simple way that this could be remedied, and so that was what I finally did. When Vera was out of the city and away from home on business, as she was half the time, I went on the prowl to reassert my own identity.

Men aren't that easy to find for a single girl. There are places that a woman on her own can't easily go, which is why females so often hunt in pairs. Two girls can go to a bar or to the movies, but it isn't so easy for one. I tried both, knowing I was bound to attract men – and I did, but not the kind I was interested in.

Nor did I want to be mistaken for a hooker; I didn't want to become involved with any guy who wanted me simply for sex – because even though that was all I was really after, it would have meant meeting him on his terms. Any relationship had to abide by my rules and regulations.

I did managed to meet a different man every now and then, and we'd go off together and fuck. At his place, in his car, standing up in an alley, it didn't matter so long as I could have his cock for a few minutes. I never told them where I lived, because I didn't want them coming around or phoning up when Vera was there. Also I didn't want them to discover my address; it was one of the most expensive parts of the city, and they'd have wondered why a girl from there should have been fucking them. After we'd screwed I would never see any of them again, I'd sampled what they had to offer and that was enough – there were plenty more studs in the world.

Rules are made to be broken, and in the end I did take someone back with me to Vera's place. She'd gone away that morning and wasn't due back for a couple of days. I was feeling lonely, and all I wanted at first was someone to talk to. But cities are the loneliest places in the world, so full of people, all of them strangers. Everyone looks through you as though you don't exist, as they rush here and there, running like crazy but getting nowhere. Like caged rats in a treadmill.

I never even asked his name, but that was usually what happened. I seldom knew a guy long enough to discover what he was called, because that wasn't important. He was only about as tall as me, very skinny, and he must have been in his mid-twenties. He looked much older when I first saw him, which was while I was sitting in the park and staring at the ducks on the lake. He seemed so destitute that I could almost have imagined him snatching one of the ducks from the water and gobbling it down raw. He was wearing an old patched coat, a piece of string tied around it as a belt; his sneakers had holes in them; his brown hair was tangled, and there was a week's stubble on his chin. It was the stubble which attracted me, as I imagined it rubbing coarsely against the inside of my thighs.

He'd been glancing covertly at me for a while, and after a few minutes he came and stood next to the bench where I was sitting, watching me from the corner of his eye, and I realized that beneath all the grime he was fairly young and quite handsome. He sat down at the other end of the seat. I pretended not to notice him, but I crossed my legs and let my skirt ride high above my knee as I shifted my position, making sure that my bra-less boobs also jiggled within my tight blouse. He slid closer to me.

'Can you let me have the price of a cup of coffee?' he asked softly.

I ignored him for a couple of seconds, then slowly turned my head. 'Did you say something?' I said, in a tone which suggested that I didn't really believe he could have been talking to me.

'Can you let me have the price of a cup of coffee?' he repeated, staring at the ground between his feet.

'Coffee is very bad for your health,' I pointed out. 'It contains caffeine, and it's a stimulant.'

'Lady,' he said, and he finally turned his head to look directly at me, 'if you're that concerned about my welfare, then I'll buy a cup of tea.'

I smiled, and I opened my bag. An idea had occurred to me, and I squeezed my thighs together and clenched the muscles of my cunt in expectation. I was thinking of the man last week who'd assumed I was a prostitute, and all I'd been doing was standing on a corner and waiting for a taxi. When I'd turned him down, he'd kept offering me more money. Each time I refused, he became more angry, but he continued adding to the pile of notes in his outstretched hand. The idea of money for sex had been quite stimulating, but he'd been so ugly and repulsive that I'd simply laughed at him and walked away.

But what if I was the one who was paying?

I pulled out a wad of notes and held them loosely in my hand. If the man wanted, he could easily have snatched them and run off; but if he did that, he wasn't the sort of guy I needed and it would be best if I found out in time.

'Would that be enough?' I asked. 'You could buy both coffee and tea with that. And plenty of other things, too.'

The man stared at the money, and he licked his lips. His hand began to reach for the notes, but then he withdrew, wiping his palm across his threadbare knee.

'Don't pretend, lady,' he said angrily, and he started to rise.

'I'm not pretending,' I told him, and he hesitated, turning to look at me again. 'This isn't a gift. I'm not giving it to you for nothing. You're going to have to earn it. But if you do the job properly, it's all yours.'

He leaned back against the seat, glancing around the park as if to ensure we couldn't be overheard. 'What do you want?'

'I want you,' I told him.

He frowned, not understanding.

'I want you to fuck me,' I added.

He stared at me, his eyes blinking rapidly.

'You know what a fuck is, don't you?' I asked. 'It's when you stick your cock into my cunt. Could you do that?'

The man scratched at his stubbled jaw, his eyes focused on the money, then he looked me up and down. 'I might be able to do that for you,' he told me. 'What's the catch? Your old man been playing around and you want some action yourself for revenge? Your husband going to shoot my knob off?'

'There's no catch,' I assured him. 'This is a simple business proposition. You fuck me, I pay you. I'm not married, you don't have to worry about any other man. No one's going to shoot your prick off, though depending how good it tastes I might try to bite it off.' I uncrossed my legs, spreading them wide, my hand resting on my lap, fingers lightly tapping my crotch. 'What do you say?'

He shrugged. 'Could do,' he agreed casually, but there was a hint of a smile at the corners of his mouth 'I'll have to check my diary. When do you want to be fucked?'

'How about now?'

He glanced around. 'What? Here?'

That presented a problem. The guy obviously didn't have a place of his own or a car, and we were in the middle of a busy public area in daylight. But I was

123

feeling so randy by this time that there was only one choice open to me – and twenty minutes later we were in Vera's apartment.

'This is quite a place you've got here,' the man said, staring around, but in admiration rather than envy.

'It's okay,' I agreed. 'How about that cup of coffee you were asking for?' I led the way towards the kitchen.

'That'll be fine,' he said, and he sat down by the table as I reached for the percolator. 'You were serious, weren't you?' he added.

'About what?'

'About me fucking you?'

'Of course,' I said. 'Why? Don't you believe me? Why did you come with me?'

'I wasn't sure if I believed you or not at first,' he told me.

'And now?'

He shook his head doubtfully. 'I'm even more uncertain.'

I shrugged, as though all this was perfectly reasonable. 'Why?'

'It's not the kind of offer I get every day.'

'There's a first time for everything,' I said.

'Are you one of those crazy kinky rich girls who gets their kicks from bums like me?'

'Are there such women?'

'I don't know,' he said. 'But I've always hoped there were!' He laughed, shaking his head in amused bewilderment.

I laughed also. 'Tell you what,' I told him, 'to prove I meant what I said back in the park . . .' I didn't finish my sentence in words but with actions – I stripped off. Standing in the kitchen, in front of the man I'd just picked up, I quickly shed my clothes. It didn't take long, because I'd been wearing absolutely nothing beneath my skirt and blouse, which I simply let fall and lie on the floor.

My visitor stared, his eyes popping.

'You still want some coffee?' I asked, allowing my hand to drop to my pubis, idly twisting at my brown curls.

Slowly, he shook his head. 'Perhaps later,' he said very quietly.

'Much later, I hope,' I said, moving towards him, sitting down on his knee and putting one arm around his neck, my free hand feeling for his cock – then finding it already half erect and helping it to rise even more.

'Ah . . . listen,' he said, his eyes gazing at my hand. 'I'm not all that clean at the moment. I've been living rough and I haven't changed my clothes or had a chance to wash for a long while, so I know I must stink a bit. Do you want me to take a bath first?'

I shook my head. 'No, I want you exactly the way you are – or will be as soon as we get these off you.' I began to remove his dirty old clothes, climbing off his knee for a few seconds while I slipped his pants down, then resuming my position.

His hands went to my breasts, stroking and fondling them; his fingers were filthy, there was dirt behind the nails, and he left grubby streaks across my flesh. I stroked my face against his chin, the stubble scratching my flesh. He'd been right, he did stink. It was the smell of stale masculine sweat, and to me it was the most exotic perfume I'd ever inhaled. I ran my fingers across his firm cock then stroked his dangling balls, then I slid off his lap and nuzzled my head between his legs. Here the odour was even stronger, and the brutal smell of his raw maleness was absolutely irresistible. I had to have him, and my mouth opened to engulf the first few inches of his prick, sucking and licking at his proud manhood.

I guzzled for perhaps a minute before unwillingly tearing my lips and tongue away. I didn't want to bring him off too soon, because my cunt was aching for his length.

Standing up, I grabbed his tool in one hand and led

125

him back along the corridor. I hesitated outside my door, then moved on to Vera's room. Her bed was bigger, more interesting, and I wanted to be properly fucked by a real man in there.

My lover-to-be gazed at the black bedroom, the mirrored ceiling, the pin-ups, the weapons, the hunting trophies, but he said not a word. I let go of his tool and pointed to the circular bed.

'Lie down,' I ordered, and he obeyed.

Once he was on the bed, I pulled the top cover over him, folding his body inside and hiding him completely except for his erect knob. It wasn't that I didn't want to see him, rather that he had only one vital piece of equipment – which was the single reason why I needed him.

His cock was still wet and shiny with my saliva, and I climbed onto the bed and stood above it, gripping the pink member and holding it vertical, slowly lowering myself onto its bold rigidity. I groaned with pleasure as his prick slid deep into my twat, and I didn't move for several seconds, simply enjoying the perfect sensation of warm flesh within my flesh.

Then the man moved; his hand appeared from beneath the cover, and he manoeuvred his face free.

'I was suffocating under there,' he said. 'Is it okay if I breathe, or were you planning on going in for necrophilia?'

'Shut up and fuck me,' I told him.

And he did.

When Vera walked in, neither of us had yet climaxed.

This was getting to be a habit. The first time was being discovered fucking Mr Compton at school, later I'd been caught by Jerry with his father's cock in my mouth. I should have learned from those experiences, and maybe I did: I was expelled from school; my relationships with both Jerry and Edward were broken. And this time it meant that Vera and I were through – which was what I'd really wanted. I was fed up with

126

being at her beck and call every moment, of living in her shadow.

Without knowing what I was doing, a part of me had planned for this to occur. I'd been aware that Vera was due back after only one day, although I'd convinced myself she would be gone twice as long and that it would be safe to bring someone back with me. A man. To Vera's bed. To fuck.

I was glad it happened, glad she discovered us, glad I was thrown out. If I hadn't escaped from Vera, I could have been trapped with her for years.

It was my partner who noticed her first. He was above me, and his eyes must have turned towards the door as it swung open. I didn't realize until he became still. I'd been staring into the mirror above me, watching his buttock muscles tense and relax as he screwed into me. Watching myself being shafted added a whole new dimension to my pleasure. It was like being a voyeur, peeping through a keyhole to watch another couple fucking away, their bodies moving in harmony, speckled with sweat.

When he suddenly stopped moving, I thought for a moment that he was going to shoot his spunk into me, and I waited for the hot gush of come splashing against the walls of my vulva. But then I noticed the direction of his gaze, and in the mirror I saw Vera standing in open-mouthed astonishment.

She dashed across to the bed and attacked me. She took no notice of the man, who swiftly withdrew his embedded prick and tried to restrain her. Vera was possessed by insane fury. She thumped and punched and scratched and clawed at me, screaming and raving at the top of her voice.

'You filthy whore . . . ! You dirty slut . . . ! You stinking tramp . . . ! You evil bitch . . . ! You . . . you . . . you . . . you . . . scheming ungrateful miserable rotten . . . cunt!'

I managed to roll aside and get to the other side of the bed, and the man at last grasped Vera firmly around

127

the torso, pinning her arms to her side. She froze immediately, in absolute horror and shock as she felt the warm stiffness of his knob pressed hard against her back, and her expression became even wilder. With a swift twist and turn, she burst free and stepped away.

'Get away from me!' she warned the man, pointing with a threatening finger. 'You've got ten seconds to leave my house, both of you. Or else you're dead!' She'd backed up against the wall which held her array of weapons, and she glanced meaningfully at the lethal display.

I made for the door, and the guy was close behind me. We raced into the kitchen for our things, then sped towards the front door. There was no time for me to fetch anything from my room, I didn't want to risk it – I knew when Vera was serious; and in this case she was deadly serious. All I took with me was my skirt, my blouse, my shoes, my bag.

We dashed out and started down the stairs, leaping them three at a time, not daring to wait for the elevator. We paused briefly two flights down in order to hastily pull on our clothes, then we continued our escape.

Outside on the street, we paused for breath. The man shook his head and rolled his eyes. I thought about what had happened, and I couldn't help grinning.

'Was that your mother?' the guy asked, and I grinned even more. 'Don't suppose you're going to pay me now, are you?' he added.

'You haven't fulfilled your part of the bargain,' I said.

'But I fucked you,' he claimed.

'Fucking includes orgasm,' I pointed out. 'I could have finger-fucked myself to the same effect. I wanted your spunk in my twat.'

'It ain't my fault we were interrupted.' He sighed. 'Just when I was beginning to enjoy myself, too. Ah, well.' He shrugged and began to walk away.

'Hold on,' I told him. 'Where're you going?' I hurried to catch up with him.

'Back to the park,' he answered.

'You live there?'

He nodded. 'Got a nice secluded hollow beneath some trees. Why? You've been thrown out of home – does that mean you want to come and live with me?' He smiled at the notion.

'Not exactly. I was just wondering where we could go so you could finish off screwing me.' I didn't intend to let him escape. He'd taken me halfway to the ultimate peak, now he had to guide me all the way to the top.

He paused and stared into my eyes, to see if I was serious. I met his level gaze without blinking.

'Let's go back to my place,' he suggested. 'I got lots of room.'

'The park?'

'The park,' he repeated. 'You ever fucked in the open air, with the grass and the dirt beneath you, the wind blowing against your naked body? It's great, I tell you.'

He was right, it was great.

The sunlight cast shadows on our nude bodies as we rolled over and over together, hidden from the other people in the park by nothing more than a few branches and a screen of leaves. As we fucked, we could hear cyclists go riding by a few feet away; joggers panting past our hiding place; people walking slowly along and peering through the thick foliage; kids playing football nearby, all the time with the threat that the ball would come bursting into the small clearing or someone would take a short cut or come to investigate the noise, and we'd be caught once again.

The danger of discovery added to the fun, as did what was for me the unique sensation of fucking outdoors, of getting back to nature, of feeling the hard earth beneath my back as the stranger drove his rigid cock into me, trying to screw me into the ground.

After so much waiting, it didn't take me long to

achieve my first juddering orgasm. Less than a minute later, my partner came, flooding my womb with his hot seed and triggering a second and even more wonderful climax deep inside me.

After fucking, usually I'd quickly pull on my clothes, or whatever I'd removed; so would the guy who'd just shafted me, then we'd go our separate ways. Now I had nowhere to go, yet this hollow in the park was my lover's home, and so we lay side by side in each other's arms. I drifted into a luxurious slumber, the man's warm body pressed against me.

But when I awoke, I was cold – and alone.

The guy had disappeared, and with him had gone my bag and all it contained.

At least he hadn't stolen my clothes, but that was all he'd left me – apart from the souvenirs of our fucking: the dried smear of crystallized spunk which had trickled from my cunt and onto my thigh, the dirty marks from his hands and the ground which were all over my body.

What the guy had done was typical. You have to keep your eyes on men all the time, they can't be trusted. They'll fuck your body, then they'll screw you for whatever else they can steal.

I ran my hands all over myself, brushing off the loose earth and grass, picking the twigs and leaves out of my hair. I slipped into my skirt and blouse, then pulled on my shoes. It was getting late, growing dark. I had no money, nowhere to go.

There was no way I could have returned to Vera even if I'd wanted to. I had only two real choices – I could sell myself for a job, or I could sell my body for sex.

Which turned out to be very much the same.

Chapter Eleven

I left the park and turned the corner, crossing over into one of the city's busiest streets. The first place I came to, I decided, I'd go in and ask for a job. But the building on the corner turned out to be a restaurant, and so I hesitated. I'd worked as a waitress, so it would have been easy to do it again; but I'd had enough of restaurants. If I had to work, there was no point doing something which would bore me from the first minute. I might as well try something different, even if the novelty only lasted a few hours.

What I needed was a job which would also give me somewhere to live, and as I studied the buildings which stretched ahead of me I saw exactly the kind of place I was looking for. It was a hotel, and I was aware that they often had staff accommodation because various kinds of employees had to be available there at all hours of the day and night. Maybe I could work behind the bar. I'd done that sometimes at Edward's, and it had been better than waitressing.

I walked on towards the hotel. It occurred to me that they might not want any staff, but I decided to be positive. I'd have to persuade them that they needed me, and I'd become very good at convincing people to do as I wished – one particular sort of people, that was: the male sort . . .

It was quite a large old hotel, five floors high, and I paused outside and studied my reflection in the glass doors to make sure I didn't look too bedraggled. Then I entered the wide foyer and walked towards the reception desk.

'Can I help you?' asked the blonde girl, dressed in a smart uniform with the hotel name stitched to the pocket of her jacket.

'Yes,' I replied. 'I've come about the job.'

Her professional smile vanished, replaced by a frown. 'Job? What job?'

'The one advertised in the paper,' I said.

She shook her head doubtfully. 'I don't know anything about that. Are you sure?'

'Of course I'm sure,' I told her. 'That's why I'm here. Someone must know about it. Can I see the manager?' I smiled at her.

'Mr Moss isn't here now,' she said. 'But there's the assistant manager, Mr Saville, I suppose he must know about it.' She reached for the telephone and punched out a number, but there was no reply. 'He doesn't seem to be in his office at present.'

'Why don't you tell me where his office is?' I suggested. 'Then I can go and wait for him?' I smiled again. It never hurts to smile, and it can work wonders – even with a woman.

The receptionist nodded, pointing to the far end of the foyer. 'You see that corridor there? Go along as far as you can, turn left, and it's one of the doors on the right. There's a sign to say which office it is. You can't miss it.'

'Thanks,' I said. 'What's it like working here?'

She shrugged, pursing her lips. 'It's better than some jobs I've had. But it's like any work, it depends if it suits you or not, and what you get out of it.'

'Yes, you're right,' I agreed. 'What about this Mr Saville . . . ?'

The girl glanced around, leaning over the desk towards me and lowering her voice. 'Be careful you don't get too close,' she said softly. 'Watch out for his hands. You know what I mean?'

I nodded conspiratorially. 'I know,' I agreed. 'Thanks. See you later, maybe.'

'Yes, maybe. Good luck.'

I turned and made my way towards the corridor in the far corner, then went in search of the assistant manager's office.

I found it without any trouble, and I knocked on the door. When there was no response, I tried the door handle. The door opened and I went inside to wait. It was a small office, lined with filing cabinets, half the rest of the space taken up by a desk which was too large for the room. There was a chair in front of the desk, and I sat down.

A few minutes later, the door opened.

'What are you doing here?' demanded a voice behind me. 'Who are you? What do you want?'

I turned and looked at the man. Everything about him was average, his build, his features. The only strange thing was his hair. He was in his thirties, but he wore his hair in a style which went out of fashion before he was born, slicked back against his scalp like some hero in a silent movie.

'Mr Saville?' I asked, crossing my legs and thrusting out my boobs.

He noticed me properly for the first time, realizing that he had an attractive girl in his office. When he'd first spoken, it had been his immediate response on discovering an intruder. But now he unconsciously adjusted his tie and straightened himself up, pulling in his stomach.

'That's right,' he said, going around to the other side of the desk and sitting down. 'What can I do for you?'

'I've come about the job,' I told him.

'What job?' he asked, looking puzzled. 'There isn't a job. You've been misinformed.'

I shook my head. 'There is a job,' I told him.

He leaned back in his chair, watching me. 'There might be,' he said slowly. He picked up a pen from his desk and began twisting it between his fingers. 'We have a very high rate of staff turnover. What can you do?'

I looked him straight in the eye. 'I can do anything you want, anything at all that you'd like me to do for you.'

He was tapping his teeth with the pen, its tip sliding

further into his mouth. 'The hotel trade is a service industry,' he said slowly. 'Are you good at servicing?'

'I think so.'

'What about bedrooms?' he asked. 'Are you good in bedrooms?'

From the way he mentioned 'servicing' and 'bedrooms' it was easy for me to know what kind of guy he was. He was the sort of man who got a mild sexual thrill out of making vaguely dirty innuendoes to women. He'd been looking at my body more than he had my face, which was a strong clue to a chauvinist belief that women were only there for the benefit of men. And because of the receptionist's warning to me about not letting him get too close, I knew he must have been a toucher as well. Probably not one of the men who would grab my tits, but the sort who would brush past my body in a doorway. I could handle him.

'What do you mean?' I asked, pretending I didn't know.

'We might need a chambermaid,' he explained. 'I was asking if you were any good at making beds.'

'I'm better at making out in bed,' I told him.

He blinked. 'Pardon?' he said.

'That's what you meant, isn't it?' I said. 'If I was any good at fucking?'

He shook his head rapidly, not knowing what to say. He pulled the cap off his pen and stared down at a piece of paper on his desk. 'Have you ever worked in a hotel before?' he asked, scrawling a note on the paper.

'No.'

He glanced up at me, waiting for me to say something else, to invent a story about how I was sure I was capable of doing the work, that I'd always wanted to be employed in a hotel, and I'd be ever so grateful and humble if he could see his way to letting me have a job.

'What about qualifications?' he said. 'Have you got any qualifications?'

'I'd never had any complaints about my qualifications,' I told him.

He kept watching me. 'Well,' he prompted, 'what are your qualifications?'

I unbuttoned my blouse and slipped it off my shoulders. 'These are two of them,' I told him, glancing down at my bare breasts. 'I'd have thought these were good enough to get me any job.'

The assistant manager licked at his lips. 'Have you – er – any further proof?' he wanted to know.

I stood up, and I hiked my skirt up around my waist, giving him an eyeful of my dark and curlies. Then something occurred to me, and I unfastened the garment and let it fall to the ground next to my blouse.

Mr Saville also rose, beginning to walk past me. I saw he was holding a key in his hand, about to lock the door; but I moved to stand in front of him.

'What about the job?' I asked.

'You've got it,' he said, and one hand tentatively reached out to touch my left breast.

I allowed him that, letting his fingertips stroke the nipple, which almost immediately responded and became stiff.

'What sort of job?' I asked.

'Let me lock the door,' he said urgently, his hand dropping away; he looked over my shoulder as though someone was about to burst in.

'What sort of job?' I repeated, not moving.

'Relief staff,' he said quickly. 'Helping out where you're needed. As a chambermaid, or with room service, or in the kitchens. A bit of everything.'

'I need to live in,' I said.

He shook his head. 'Impossible.'

I reached down towards his crotch, finding his stiffening prick and giving it a squeeze. 'Not for you, it isn't,' I said.

'Why don't we . . ?' He gestured with his head back towards the far side of his room.

'Fuck? Is that what you mean? Or would you rather

135

I sucked your cock? I'm very good at that. There's plenty of time, or there will be when I work here. And I'll be around more if I have a room of my own here.'

'Okay, okay, you've got one,' he said rapidly.

'And I need some cash, an advance on my pay.'

He shook his head. 'That isn't company policy.'

'What about your policy, Mr Saville?' I asked him, and now my fingers began to undo his zip.

'Okay, okay, that too.'

I let go of him, leaning back against the door. 'So I've got a job, I've got a room, and I've got some cash?'

'That's right.'

I stepped away from the door, moving past the assistant manager and picking up my clothes. 'Then I think I'd like to go up to my room. I've had a busy day, and I'm tired. I've got to work tomorrow, you know.'

The man simply stared at me. 'But . . .'

'That comes later. If I stay on here, and if everything works out, then maybe I'll let you shove your cock in my cunt. Or maybe I'll just suck and suck it until your spunk shoots out all over my face. Would you like that?'

He nodded, blinking. 'Why not . . . now?'

'Because, Mr Saville, you might decide to fuck me and then conveniently forget about the contract of employment which we've just negotiated.'

'If you think you can walk in here and talk your way into a job with . . . with vague promises of letting me . . . have an affair with you, then you've got another think coming,' he announced abruptly. He zipped himself up and then pointed to the door. 'Just get out of here!'

I shrugged. 'If I do, then you'll never get the chance to fuck me.'

The man's pointing finger wavered.

'You've got a job, so why not give it to me?' I said. 'You've nothing to lose – but you might have a lot to gain.' I was still holding my clothes over my arm, and I stepped towards the door. 'But if you want me to leave, I will. I'll go running down the corridor, scream-ing, saying that you tore my clothes off.'

'That won't do you any good,' the man said icily, trying to pretend that he wasn't concerned. 'Who'd believe you?'

'It wouldn't do the hotel's reputation much good,' I said. 'Think of the bad publicity. I could say you tried to rape me. You've got a hard-on, Mr Saville, which means that there's probably a drop of spunk oozing from the tip of your cock this very second. The police forensic investigation would discover that, they'd believe me.' I wasn't at all sure that anyone would believe me, or even if I'd have the nerve to sprint nude through the hotel; but I guessed that the assistant manager wasn't prepared to call my bluff – and I was right.

'Ah . . . well . . . now . . . er . . . let's not be too hasty about this, huh? Why don't you just put your clothes back on, then we can talk this over like reasonable people?'

He watched anxiously as I dressed again.

'Where's my room?' I asked.

The man went to sit behind his desk, and he picked up the telephone and pressed a couple of buttons. 'Hello? Yes, Mr Saville here. Could you ask Mrs Potter to come down to my office? Yes. I've just hired a new girl, and I want her to be taken to her room. Thank you.' He hung up again. 'Satisfied?' he asked.

I nodded, and I was aware that in a strange way the assistant manager was also satisfied with what had happened. He liked being pushed around, dominated by a woman; and he could also console himself with the thought that I might keep to my side of the bargain and let him fuck me.

And it was true – I might. He had a cock, and that was all I ever needed.

I didn't feel guilty at manipulating him. The guy in the park had taken advantage and used me, so I was simply claiming my revenge against the male species.

But even in the park it hadn't been all one-sided. My temporary lover might have stolen my bag and my money, but at least he'd given me a couple of climaxes in exchange.

A minute later there was a knock on the door, and a small plump woman of about fifty rolled in.

'This is Mrs Potter,' the assistant manager said to me, 'she'll show you to your room.' He glanced at the woman. 'This is the new girl, Mrs Potter. Take care of her, will you? She'll be filling in at first, wherever we need her, and we'll see where she's most suitable. Thank you.'

The woman looked at me, but said nothing. She gestured towards the door with a flick of her head, and I followed her out of the room. I glanced back at Mr Saville, who was watching me leave, and I blew him a kiss. Then I shut the door, and Mrs Potter led me up several flights of twisting, creaking stairs to a distant wing of the ancient hotel.

'This is your room,' she said at last, reaching a doorway at the end of a narrow landing. 'You'll be sharing it with Claire. I'll see you later about what work you're doing. We start at six o'clock tomorrow morning.' As she spoke, she produced a huge key ring and unhooked one of the keys. She handed it to me, then turned away and went back the way we'd come.

I tried the door handle. The door was unlocked, and I pushed it open an inch then tapped my knuckles against it, as a warning to anyone inside. I heard a noise from within, it sounded familiar but I couldn't place it for a moment. But as soon as I stepped inside, I recalled the sound.

The room was very small, made even smaller by its sloping ceiling; it must have been right up in the roof of the hotel. There were two single beds on opposite walls, and lying on top of one of them was a naked girl with long black hair – and a vibrator up her cunt.

Her eyes were shut and she hadn't heard me because of the noise her penis-shaped vibrator was making.

But suddenly she opened her eyes and saw me, and her mouth fell open.

'Hello,' I said, 'you must be Claire. This my bed over here?'

I didn't want the girl to feel embarrassed so I walked towards the other bed, and in moments I'd stripped off my clothes and was lying down, my legs wide apart, two fingers rubbing against my clitoris.

'It's the most relaxing way to finish off a day, I always find,' I added, sighing and rubbing my free hand across my breasts.

Claire nodded her head uncertainly. The vibrator was still deep inside her, trembling away. She spoke at last. 'I don't – um – usually – ah – that is . . .'

'Oh, I do,' I assured her. 'All the time. If I can't find a cock to do it for me.'

We lay four feet apart, masturbating ourselves; but I could tell Claire had lost interest and felt uncomfortable with me there. She was an attractive girl of about twenty, with delicious looking dark nipples which I longed to feel between my lips. I wanted to go over to her, to take control of her vibrator and bring her off, to force her head between my thighs and sense her warm wet tongue thrusting deep into my twat.

Vera had shown me what a woman's affection could be like, and I yearned to try out what she'd taught me on another girl. I still had no idea what a cunt tasted like.

But it was far too early to make such a move towards Claire, so instead I continued to lie where I was, and I simply imagined what we could have been doing to each other. And as we were sharing a room, my wish was bound to come true before too long.

Meanwhile I watched the vibrator shaft as it shuddered inside Claire's twat, and studied her jet black curls and smooth soft flesh. I gave myself an exquisite orgasm, but I'm sure that Claire faked hers – and I intended to rectify that also in due time.

The girl was a chambermaid and she talked to me

about hotel work, giving me hints and tips about the job. I liked Claire, she told a good story and made me laugh. She was also interested in my favourite topic – sex.

'You get to see lots of men in this line of work,' she said. 'And you get to see all of them, in some cases. Most of them are real perverts, aren't they? I knock at the door before entering, so I can make up the bed, and they shout out "Come in" – and the number of times a guy's been stark naked, you wouldn't believe. And not just the young ones, but really old guys. Old and skinny, nothing but bones, or old and fat, ones with such big bellies that they can't have seen their dicks for years – but they make sure that I can see it. I think they believe it's a magic wand, just the sight of it is enough to make a girl peel off her clothes and collapse on the bed, legs wide apart.'

'You get propositioned directly, do you?' I asked.

'Sometimes. But more often they get their kicks out of flashing, showing off a limp dick or their hard-on. I once even had a guy jerking himself off into the basin while I was making the bed.'

'What did you do?'

'Pretended to ignore him,' said Claire. 'Then I slipped away and fucked myself with the neck of an empty wine bottle.'

I thought what a pity it had been empty; I'd like to have drunk out of it.

'You get them reading dirty magazines,' she continued, 'or leaving them lying around so they can watch your reaction when you see them. There's something about hotels that seems to attract weirdos. Or maybe it's just because the men are away from home, in a strange city, and they don't know where to get fucked.'

'You ever accepted any of these propositions?'

Claire grinned. 'What do you think? You know what it's like when you're feeling horny as hell, then suddenly you've got the chance of being screwed –

140

there's plenty of opportunity in this job. And not just from the guests.'

'Mr Saville?' I suggested.

'Greasy? I wouldn't touch him if he had the last knob in the world. Gives me the creeps, he does.' Claire shuddered. We were still nude, sitting opposite one another as we chatted. The girl's legs were drawn up and she hugged her knees; but her feet were spread and I had a lovely detailed view of her cunt. It was the first time I'd seen another girl's vagina, and I found it fascinating. There had been occasional glimpses of Vera's shaven twat, but that was all. Until now I'd only been able to study my own labia and clitoris, holding a mirror between my thighs.

'Anyhow,' Claire continued, 'the funniest thing is when you walk in on a couple who are fucking away. They're making so much noise that they can't hear you knock on the door.' She paused for a moment, grinning. 'I know what that feeling's like now, because of you.'

'A man and a woman fucking, you mean?'

Claire nodded. 'I've never seen a couple of guys at it, and I don't think I'd want to.' She shook her head and pulled a face. 'Do you like having anal sex? You know, up the ass? The idea makes me squirm.'

'I've tried it,' I said, 'because I think everything ought to be sampled at least once, but I didn't think much of it. I didn't enjoy it as much as having a prick in my mouth, for example. And why use your rear when that's what your cunt's for? It's just a waste of a prick and all that spunk.'

'Yeah, that's what I think,' Claire agreed. 'And talking of spunk, when you've got a couple sharing a bed, with a bit of luck they'll fuck and stain the sheets. Then you might get a tip, because they feel so guilty about leaving a mess.' She licked her lips and stared at me, as though wondering whether to tell me something. 'Sometimes I've found sheets still damp with spunk, and I've pulled down my briefs and climbed into bed, rubbing my cunt across the stickiness and imagined that I was being screwed. And I've climaxed almost at once.'

I saw her inner labia swell slightly and begin to moisten as she spoke, and her pink clit stiffened; I felt my own genitals do the same and start to moisten. Claire reached for the vibrator that was by her side.

'Do you mind?' she asked.

I shook my head. 'Not if you'll let me use it after you,' I said.

She smiled and switched the thing on, stroking its plastic glans against her wet cunt lips.

As I watched, I was also thinking about what I should do. Not immediately, but before too long.

After being abandoned in the park earlier, I was left with absolutely nothing – less than I'd had before Vera picked me up and drove me into the city. Now I was on my way again. Vera had shown me that there was more to life than working, or that at least one should have some material wealth and luxury to show for it. I'd been her sex slave and had shared her apartment; she'd been good to me, but others could be better. I was able to twist men around my finger – or my clit.

The hotel job it would only be temporary, I knew. Vera had pointed the way, and I was heading up. Nothing was going to stop me.

But the one thing I wasn't looking forward to was six o'clock tomorrow morning, when work began.

Chapter Twelve

It took me four days before I came across my first naked man in one of the hotel rooms – one who wasn't naked because it was me who'd stripped off his clothes . . .

The first day at work I happened to let slip the fact that I'd previously been a waitress, and so naturally I was assigned to the dining room. As I took orders, served meals and cleared empty dishes away, I thought that I might just as well have applied for a job in that restaurant I'd seen. But that would have still meant finding somewhere to stay, and at least in the hotel I'd met up with Claire.

We'd been out together two evenings, and I wished I'd known her before. Claire had such a bubbly extrovert personality that she attracted guys like a magnet, and both times we each scored. The first evening was with a couple of salesmen who were in the city for a conference, and they took us back to their hotel rooms – luckily or not, they weren't staying in the hotel where we worked.

We had a terrific time. I know I did, and Claire claimed the same. We'd started off in a bar, gone to a disco, followed by a nightclub, and only then had we ended up back at their hotel. My guy was a tall ginger-haired man, with a thick beard. Our escorts thought they'd made the choice, but Claire and I decided which one each of us would have. I picked him because I wanted to find out if his hair was ginger all over – and it was. His whole body was covered in a mass of reddish hair, his arms and legs, his chest, even his shoulder blades, and his cock was like a sturdy tree growing from a forest of ginger curls. But what I liked best was the way his beard tickled my thighs and the hairs of his moustache caressed my labia as he demon-

143

strated his mastery of cunnilingus on my appreciative cunt.

The second time we met two teenage football fans who'd arrived in the city to support their team in the next day's match. They stopped us in the street to ask directions, but that was just a pretext to pick us up. They had very little money and nowhere to stay, and so we smuggled them up to our room at the top of the hotel. It was cramped enough in there with just Claire and I, but with four of us we could hardly move – though we managed to move enough . . .

It was the first time I'd ever been in a room where other people were fucking, or had any witnesses to my own carnal adventures. But it was very enjoyable. We were all drunk, and we did our best to keep quiet so that we wouldn't be overheard. The more we tried to be silent, the more noise we made. One of us would start to giggle, and the others would become infected with a severe bout of laughter. The beds creaked, our damp bodies slapped wetly together, and Claire and I both cried out as we came.

I found it very stimulating to watch Claire being screwed over in the other bed, and I noticed how the two guys were fucking in unison – both thrusting in and pulling out simultaneously. They didn't seem to be doing it deliberately, but seeing the other couple was like watching a mirror image of me and my own lover.

We didn't try a foursome or a threesome or anything like that; it was just plain screwing, one to one. After we'd been fucked, however, the two guys changed places – and partners. His cock was still wet from Claire's twat, the second teenager drilled straight into me and within a couple of minutes I'd achieved my second climax.

That's the thing about younger men, they mightn't have the style or technique – but they've got the stamina. Even after squirting out a good throw of come, they could keep their pricks up and were ready for more action.

Apart from Mark, those two were the youngest guys I'd ever screwed . . . but even so they were at least a couple of years older than I was.

We fucked well into the night, until we all fell asleep through an excess of alcohol and semen.

It was the next day that I began working as a chambermaid, on the same floor as Claire and under her guidance.

If a guest was leaving that day, they had to check out by eleven, and we did the room afterwards. If they were staying on, we'd do it earlier in the morning. The routine was to knock on the door and wait, using the pass key to enter if there was no reply. And if there was a reply, we'd either go in or return later, depending on what the guest wanted.

I'd already done four rooms, and when I knocked on the fifth a man's voice from inside yelled: 'Come on in, it's open!'

So I opened the door and went in. Then I heard the voice again: 'Come on through into the bathroom, honey!'

It seemed a reasonable enough request, so I crossed the room and pushed open the connecting door. There was a man lying in the bath, naked. Or naked apart from a pair of thick rimmed glasses. That in itself wasn't so surprising, but the unusual thing was that there was no water in the bath; I could tell there had been until a few minutes ago, because the bath was streaked with drops of water and his body was still damp. He was about fifty, with more hair on his chest than his head. And he also had an enormous erection.

He was facing away from me, but he saw my reflection in the steamed up mirror on the far wall.

'Will you start by sucking my knob, honey?' he suggested.

'I usually start by making the bed,' I told him, and I began to turn away.

He looked around swiftly, seeing me and my hotel uniform. His eyes widened in amazement, his hands dropping to cover his stiff prick as best they could.

'Oh, no,' he groaned. 'I'm sorry, honey, I'm really sorry.'

I paused, looking back at him.

'I thought you were someone else,' the man explained quickly. 'That's why I . . .' He shook his head, lost for words.

'That's okay,' I said, because I could tell he was telling the truth. 'I've seen a cock or two in my time. Would you like me to turn the cold shower on? Looks as though you need it.' I gestured to the shower head above the bath.

'That isn't what I need,' he muttered.

I could guess what he meant. 'Who were you expecting?' I asked.

He hesitated, glancing up at me and wondering why I was still there. He shrugged. 'A masseuse,' he said. 'Two of them. A couple of girls who offer a visiting massage service. You know what that is?'

I nodded. He was talking about a dial-a-fuck organization. 'Isn't it a bit early for that kind of thing?'

He smiled. 'Don't pretend, honey You know these kind of things can't be done by the clock. Anyhow, I like it in the morning. I'm not as young as I used to be, and I feel tired and don't appreciate it as much later on.' He stared down at himself, still vainly trying to keep every millimetre of cock flesh hidden from my eyes even though I'd already seen it. 'I wake up with a terrific hard-on, so it seems a shame for me to waste it. That's why I phoned up the massage parlour. Twenty-four hour service, it says. I hope that doesn't mean they take twenty-four hours to get here!' He laughed briefly.

'Perhaps I can help you,' I offered.

He glanced back at me, his face suspicious, thinking

this was some kind of joke or trick. 'What do you mean?'

'What does a massage involve exactly?' I asked. 'I start off by sucking your cock, that's what you said. That sounds more appealing to me than cleaning up your bedroom.'

'Well – ah – massage is just a polite word for fucking, I suppose. That's how I like it to end up. But all kinds of things can happen before then. There have to be two girls, I need two girls.'

He obviously thought a lot of himself, but I didn't say so. His penis was big, but I'd seen bigger – and been fucked by bigger.

'Why are you lying in the bath without any water?' I asked, which to me was the strangest thing of all.

'I had my first orgasm in the bath,' he answered, as though that explained everything.

'Someone was sucking your knob at the time?' I asked.

He noticed I was smiling, and he shook his head.

'It would be easier for me to do it if you were out of the bath,' I said. 'The sides are in the way, and I'd have trouble keeping my balance when I lean down.'

'Don't play games, honey.'

'I'm not,' I told him.

'I only like it to be sucked for a minute or so,' the man said. 'I don't want to shoot off too soon. At my age, I have to conserve my semen and my hard-on.' He was watching me when finally he let go of his prick, as if unleashing a wild animal and hoping to scare me away.

Instead I moved closer, standing opposite his rigid tool. 'You want me to take my clothes off?' I asked.

He looked into my face. 'Are you serious?'

I nodded.

'I need two girls, honey,' he said, and I could tell he didn't really believe me.

'I'm as good as two girls.'

'I'm sure you are,' he agreed, nodding. 'But are you double-jointed?'

I frowned, not understanding.

'You can't lick your own cunt, can you?' he explained. 'And that's what I like to see. That's why I need two girls. I like to watch them go to work on each other.' He started to stand up, but I put my hand on his shoulder.

'How much do you usually pay for this?' I asked.

The man named a price, and I tried not to show any reaction. It was as much as I'd earn at the hotel in a fortnight.

'That's each, of course,' he added.

'Of course,' I echoed, hiding my astonishment. I'd considered it was a lot for two girls, but each one was paid that much . . . !

'I'm a rich man,' the guy told me. 'I don't mind admitting it. I've worked hard for thirty years, and now I have more than I can spend if I live to be a hundred. I like giving people money. If I pay well, I get satisfaction and I can make others happy. It's so easy. Just a simple thing like money, pieces of paper, and people will do anything for me. You're a chamber-maid, but I'd have left you a big tip just for cleaning up my room. I'm a generous fellow.' He nodded his head, then slowly grinned. 'I can afford to be.' He tried to climb out of the bath again, but my hand was still holding him down. 'Let me out, honey, I've enjoyed this conversation but I'm getting cold.'

'What about your penis?' I asked. 'I haven't tasted it yet, and I thought you wanted a suck.'

The man lifted my hand off his shoulder. 'Thanks, honey, but no thanks.' He stepped out of the bath. 'I know you mean well, but . . .' He shook his head sadly. 'Let me fetch my wallet, so I can show you my appreciation.' He took hold of my hand and led me back into the bedroom.

His grip was very loose, and I slipped away easily.

148

I made straight for the door, opened it, and went out into the corridor.

'Hey!' I heard the guy call, then his voice was silenced as the door slammed.

Three minutes later I opened the door again, this time not bothering to knock. The man was dressed already, wearing an expensive suit, standing in front of the mirror to fasten his tie. He saw my reflection and turned as I closed the door.

'This is Claire,' I said, nodding to the girl by my side. 'There's two of us now.'

The man walked towards us, his hand reaching for the door, and I thought he was going to send us away. But instead he turned the latch, then moved back to the middle of the room.

'My name's Philip,' he said. He looked at us both in turn and smiled. 'Why don't you both come in and make yourselves at home? Would you like a drink, or is it too early in the day?'

'It's never too early,' said Claire, who I'd fully briefed, 'for a drink of spunk.'

'I hope your cock hasn't gone down,' I said.

Philip nodded sadly. 'It has.'

'Then we'd better do something about that,' I told him, and I glanced at Claire.

She nodded, and side by side we strode purposefully towards the man. Before he had a chance to avoid us, we grabbed hold of him and flung him onto the double bed – then we began to tear off his clothes. We both made for his pants first, and we shoved and pushed at each other for the privilege of unzipping our victim. Philip struggled, pretending to be unwilling, but I could tell from his expression that he was adoring the way we were fighting over him.

I won the first battle, knocking Claire away with my shoulder as I firmly grasped Philip's zip, tugging it down and also unfastening the top of his pants. I knelt on the bed by his groin, while Claire had to content herself with pulling off the man's jacket. I reached

149

inside the zip and took hold of the major prize. As Philip had said, he'd lost his erection; but even when flaccid his cock had lost little of its magnificent size. I bent my head to kiss its tip, drawing in the first couple of inches of its soft length and circling my tongue around the ridge behind the glans. Within a couple of seconds I felt the flesh begin to harden.

But before I could do much more, Claire was dragging me off. She'd undone Philip's tie, and now she looped it around my throat and was yanking me backwards, almost strangling me. The man's dick slipped from my lips as I leaned back, and then I stumbled and fell off the end of the bed. Before I could regain my balance, Claire had taken my place and was bent over the man's crotch, her long black hair cascading down to hide all sight of both her face and Philip's prick.

I leaned forward, brushing her hair aside. Claire flinched, thinking I was going to drag her away, but all I wanted to do was watch – to look as she expertly drew Philip's cock into her mouth, her tongue stroking the stiffening shaft, her lips caressing the purple head, her fingers cupping the hairy balls.

She had stripped off the man's jacket and undone his shirt buttons, so I pulled the garment off and tugged at his shoes and socks, then whisked his pants away. All he was left with was his glasses.

He was leaning back against the pillow, his arms behind his head, luxuriating in Claire's oral attentions. There was plenty for us to share, and I went to kneel opposite her, Philip's penis between us.

I reached out one hand towards the thick cock in order to stake my claim. The end of Philip's prick was firmly engulfed in Claire's mouth, her saliva dripping down its length. She watched me warily as I gripped the base of the shaft between my thumb and forefinger, leaning closer and inching my face towards the trophy we both coveted. My probing tongue stretched out to touch the hard phallus.

And then we were both fellating Philip, our lips kissing, our teeth gently nibbling. My mouth moved up one side of his cock, and Claire's slid down the other, moving all the way to his testicles, which she sucked completely into her mouth. Meanwhile it was my turn to taste the swollen glans, which was wet from the other girl's tongue; but just as my lips descended over the head I noticed the first thick drop of spunk ooze from its tip, and I greedily lapped it up.

Claire's face was only a few inches from mine, and it came even closer as she released the man's testicles and rose to claim the end of Philip's cock again. We came to a silent agreement. I withdrew a little, so that one side of the purple glans was pressed against my mouth, and Claire's lips began to nuzzle the other side. We shared the man's prick between us. As our tongues darted out, licking all around the end of the shaft, inevitably they touched. Our mouths moved nearer, and we kissed, Philip's glans pushed hard against our lips. For a few seconds we licked and guzzled around the hard flesh, before realizing that it was in the way. So we simply raised our mouths an inch or two, and we carried on kissing.

Our teeth clashed, our lips rubbed together, our tongues advanced and retreated, exploring one another's mouths. Then we began to touch each other with our hands. I ran my fingers through Claire's long hair, she stroked my face; I felt for her breasts through her uniform, her hand rubbed between my thighs.

Philip was completely forgotten as we rolled onto the bed side by side, turning over and over while we tore at each other's clothes, ripping off the hotel uniforms, stripping down to our underwear. We paused, staring at one another, and I thought for a moment that Claire didn't want to go on. But she reached behind her back, unfastening her bra and releasing those superb breasts with the wonderful dark nipples which I'd admired so much when I first saw her.

Instantly I dived upon her, feasting myself on her hard nipples before she even had a chance to take off her panties. They tasted better than I'd ever imagined, rigid but with an inner softness, and my tongue licked at the dimpled flesh. I felt Claire's hands searching for my bra strap, unclipping it then freeing my own boobs. Her warm palms caressed my tits, pushing against the nipples and stimulating them to further stiffness, then her hands slid down the sides of my body, tugging at my briefs. But they were caught up because of the angle of my legs, so Claire simply grabbed hold of the hem and ripped the flimsy garment apart. It fell away, clinging to my other thigh, and I sensed her hand tentatively sliding towards my crotch.

Claire had been beneath me, but now she pushed me aside. I rolled onto my back and she knelt above me as she thumbed down her cotton panties, and I gazed at her pubic hairs and the fold in her flesh which led down to her cunt. It was her turn to sample my breasts, and her mouth descended upon my right boob; one of her hands stroked my left tit, while the other brushed lightly across my pubic hairs. My cunt quivered and trembled in anticipation, my whole body yearning for the brief touch of a finger against my throbbing clitoris.

I was stroking the girl's bottom, and to encourage her further explorations of my vagina, I reached down through the cleft of her buttocks towards her own cunt. The first thing my fingertips discovered was the puckered ridge of her anus, but I kept on going and then dipped into the moist valley of her twat.

Claire responded immediately. Her whole body stiffened, her head drawing back to release my nipple, and she sighed. Her fingers now found my inner labia, rubbing across the sensitive flesh. I groaned with contentment. The other girl knew where her own clitoris was, so she had no trouble locating mine, softly caressing it with the tip of her thumb. By this time my own fingers had homed in on their target of Claire's clit. Slowly, she tumbled off me, and we lay side by side, masturbating one another.

I like masturbating, but having someone else do it for me – and do it properly – was sheer bliss. As my fingers worked on Claire's wet cunt, it was almost as if I was fingering myself.

Our bodies pressed together, and we kissed, our lips gently sucking and chewing, tongues softly caressing. We would have been touching one another from head to toe, except for the way our busy hands kept our cunts apart.

Our cunts were the factor which we most had in common, but they weren't in contact with each other. That was what I wanted. We didn't really need our fingers on one another's clits, we could still bring ourselves off. I withdrew my hand, taking hold of Claire's wrist and dragging her away from my vagina. She gazed at me doubtfully, her mouth still locked against mine, but seemed to realize that I knew what I was doing. I pulled my lips free, gave her one more kiss of reassurance, then I began to twist away, parting my legs even more as I did so and forcing Claire to do the same.

We intertwined our thighs, opening them wide as I moved completely the other way around. Our heads were pointing in opposite directions, but one of Claire's legs was between mine, one of mine between hers – and we pushed our damp cunts together, my labia and clitoris stroking against hers.

We only had to move very slowly, enjoying the rapturous sensation, feeling the warmth swiftly building up within us. It began as a single spark, but soon grew to a hot flame, rapidly developing into a blazing fire – and finally it engulfed both of us in an orgasmic inferno, which left us sweating and gasping for breath. Our cunt juices ran freely, mingling where our pubic hairs clung wetly together.

Although I could have stayed there forever, my twat glued with come to the other girl's vaginal lips, I still hadn't achieved my ambition to actually taste a cunt, to run my tongue deep into a vulva, to suck on a clitoris. And I was aware that this was the best opportunity likely to come my way for a long time.

With some reluctance, I disentangled my legs and slid further up the bed, my face reaching the level of Claire's crotch. She was lying on her side and one of her legs was raised and bent at the knee, as if to admit some cooling air. She made no attempt to stop me as I rested my cheek on her thigh and stared into the moist folds of her gaping pink twat. I pushed my face closer, scenting the sweet smell of her femininity, my mouth opening, my tongue stretching out, its tip just touching the stiffness of her clitoris and watching it quiver.

At the same time I felt Claire's hands pulling my hips nearer to her and forcing my own thighs apart, and her mouth closed over my cunt.

We licked and sucked and ate each other, lips rubbing against labia, tongues against clits. And it was delicious, everything I'd dreamed of and more. My whole body trembled as though caught up in an earthquake, and at the same time I could feel Claire also shaking, her hips pushing hard against my mouth as she urged my tongue ever deeper. We climaxed together, my mouth flooding with her come while her own tongue lapped at my orgasmic juices.

'That looks very nice,' I heard a voice say. 'What about my turn?'

I pulled my head from Claire's cunt, licking my lips, and I gazed at Philip. I'd almost forgotten him. He'd sat quietly at the other end of the bed, watching everything we'd been doing, and now his cock was harder and bigger than ever before.

I reached out and took hold of it, feeling it throb from the pulse in the thick vein, and I rolled over onto my back, legs wide, tugging Philip's penis, aiming it towards my cunt. A good fuck was exactly what I needed.

The man fell on top of me, the end of his big knob

driving straight into my cunt; and it felt so good to have his warm solid flesh inside me. His hips jerked back and forth, my thighs and stomach slapping against his as we began to fuck.

Claire watched enviously, but she refused to be left out. She lay on her side between us, her hands stroking both of our bodies, her lips kissing us in turn. After a minute of this she grasped the man firmly around the shoulders, and by using all her strength she managed to roll Philip aside. She was probably trying to get him off me, so that she could have his prick for her own twat. But I clung tight, and as Philip fell I moved with him, and his cock remained firmly embedded inside me.

The man was on his back now, and I was squatting above, riding his thick shaft. Claire glanced at me, but from my expression she could tell that I planned to keep what I had. This was no time for sharing. One cock plus one cunt equalled ecstasy; it was the perfect mathematical equation.

Claire moved around and down, her hands going to my waist, and I thought she was trying to unseat me. But then I felt her head brush against my buttocks as her arms pushed against me, making me lean forwards so that she could squeeze her face between Philip's prick and my twat. Her wet tongue flicked out to stroke my cunt lips where the plunging shaft slid in and out, licking both my cunt and Philip's prick. And this was the ultimate in rapture – because I was having the best of both worlds, being both sucked and fucked simultaneously.

Meanwhile, as I'd bent down, the man had taken the opportunity to kiss my boobs instead of just fondling them. He pressed them against each other, forcing the nipples together until they almost touched, and he was able to draw both of them into his mouth at once, his lips and tongue working their magic upon my flesh.

Not unexpectedly, it didn't take me too long before I came again, and I cried out in triumph as the overwhelming surge of pleasure washed over me.

There's no mercy in love, and Claire used my moment of supreme fulfilment to roughly shoulder me aside, taking total possession of Philip's cock. She was holding it in her hand, a few inches from her face, and she'd just begun to manoeuvre herself so that he could fuck her – but she was too late!

Philip's prick erupted with a mighty surge of foaming spunk, which jetted from its swollen tip and splattered against the side of Claire's face. She was so surprised that she didn't react for a second, and another creamy squirt of semen hit her cheek. And then she opened her mouth wide, leaning over the bubbling glans and aiming it between her lips. The third throw accurately vanished inside her mouth, and a moment later so did the tip of Philip's knob. She sucked greedily at the still jerking penis, and I was swiftly by her side in case any should dribble from her lips.

But Claire drained the man's firm cock dry, still holding it between her lips when the organ began to lose its stiffness. Only then did the girl let go, slowly pulling her mouth back, giving the tip one final gentle kiss.

As soon as her mouth was free, I embraced her, putting my lips to her cheek – and the thick drops of come which dribbled down towards her chin. I rubbed my face across the warm liquid, smearing it all over my mouth, my tongue darting out to lick the rest of Claire's face clean and swallow down the precious creamy juice.

The girl pressed her mouth to mine, drawing in my lips sucking off the come as we kissed. I tasted semen mixed with her saliva. There were some heavy drops which I'd missed which hung beneath her chin. I wiped them off with my index finger, rolling the finger around and around so that it was totally covered with a layer of semen. I pulled my lips away from Claire's, a thin trail of spunk as fine as a spider's web stretching between us for an instant.

Glancing down to see what I was doing, I slid my spunk-laden finger deep into Claire's twat, rubbing it against her labia and across her clitoris. She groaned and writhed as I stroked her cunt – and her moans of pleasure and passionate gyrations increased even more when my tongue took the place of my finger. As I licked at the delicious mixture of cock and cunt juice, the girl climaxed once again, her thighs clamped against my head, holding my face against her vagina. I kept on licking, my tongue thrusting as deep as it could, and I sucked and swallowed everything I tasted.

Finally we unknotted our limbs and lay back on the bed, one of us either side of Philip, our damp bodies glistening. We clung close, the man's arms around us, idly stroking at our breasts and the still hard nipples.

'Okay, honeys,' he said at last. 'What would you like? Name it and it's yours.'

'Anything?' asked Claire.

'Anything,' Philip assured her. Then he grinned and added: 'Almost.'

'I'd like another orgasm,' I said.

As Philip had told me, he was a rich man; but none of his wealth had made him happy. He'd been married and divorced three times, and soon he thought his score would reach four, because he wasn't getting on very well with his latest wife.

'She just wanted me for my money, and I thought she loved me for my body,' he joked.

The only thing that he really enjoyed was the kind of performance Claire and I had given for him, and so we came to an arrangement.

When he'd asked Claire to tell him what she'd genuinely like in exchange for helping to give him the most memorable fuck he'd had in years, she told him she wanted a hotel.

I thought at first that she was kidding. After four days at the hotel, I'd had enough and couldn't wait to get away. But Claire was absolutely serious. She liked hotels, had done ever since she was a child and used to stay in them with her parents, and that was the whole reason why she worked in one. I think her secret ambition was to marry the handsome young son of the owner of a hotel chain.

I was even more surprised when Philip agreed – although not so amazed as Claire was. They soon reached an agreement whereby Philip would buy a small private hotel and give Claire a forty-nine percent share.

'I never give away more than half,' he said.

'That's okay,' I told him, 'half of your cock each means that Claire and I have all of it.'

'I hope so,' Philip said. 'I hope so.' He glanced at me. 'What about you, honey? What would you like?'

If Claire could have a hotel, I didn't feel too greedy asking for a place of my own. We made a deal whereby Philip bought the lease of a luxury apartment for me, and he agreed to take care of all the bills.

Our commitment was that in exchange Claire and I would team up once a week in order to give Philip a suck and fuck session. It seemed a reasonable enough request – and to seal the bargain we began to work on his cock between us once more, using our hands and mouths. The man claimed that he'd never be able to get it hard again so soon, but we proved him wrong. Before too long we were lying in a triangle on the bed. I had Philip's prick between my lips and Claire's tongue in my twat, while Philip himself was giving the other girl's cunt a long and languorous oral caress.

Of course our arrangement didn't last long, I never thought it could have done. I always lived for the moment, so long as I had a cock to fuck me I'd be content – and I was content most of the time.

Claire became Philip's fifth wife, but I wasn't invited on the honeymoon. I was the one who was given a wedding present, my luxury apartment in the city centre. But by this time, I had a succession of lovers. I wasn't interested in nobodies, and I made a career out of fucking the rich and the famous.

Successful men are full of drive and energy, and it's that which has taken them to the top – and the same is true of me, I suppose. When it comes to fucking, they are still determined to prove they're the best. They work long and hard hours; they fuck the same way. Long and hard. And that's the way I like it.

Some of them had their kinks, the same as anyone else. Like the government minister who insisted that I wore a studded dog collar around my neck, chained to the end of the bed, and I always had to kneel for him so that he could screw me from the rear. Or the television interviewer who would only fuck my armpit, and it had to be the left one. Or the record company tycoon who liked me to suck him off under his desk when he was sacking one of his employees. Or the famous research chemist who could only ejaculate while staring into an electron microscope as I slipped a finger into his anus. Or the brilliant young playwright who insisted that I read his manuscripts while he watched from behind a curtain and masturbated – and I didn't even have to take my clothes off. Or the judge who liked me to wear his official robes over my nude body while spanking his bare buttocks with a cane. But their fetishes hurt no one and were easily satisfied.

Sportsmen and pop stars, movie actors and politicians, industrialists and aristocrats – they were all my quarry. And always they gave me presents, little gifts to prove their affection. Such as jewellery and furs, antiques and motor cars, paintings and stocks and shares . . . even plain old money.

I soon became a rich woman. Not as rich as many of the guys I'd fucked, but rich enough to have retired if I wished and lived more than comfortably on my investments.

But why retire when I enjoyed my work and was having so much fun . . ?

Chapter Thirteen

The house was absolutely fabulous. I'd been to some amazing places in my time, but I'd never seen anything like this before. It must have been at least a mile between the gates where the security guards checked us in and the main building itself, and we drove through acres and acres of immaculately kept lawn, the narrow winding road lined on both sides by hedges which were so neat and even that they look artificial.

The building must have been one of the oldest in the whole country, a huge mansion which had been added to generation by generation, until it was now a sprawling mix of spectacularly disparate styles. Inside it was a combination of old and new, the best and most tasteful of each matched in harmony – high carved ceilings, wide marble staircases, ancient tapestries hanging on the walls; but also huge video screens, flashing laser lights, a perfect amplification system for the famous singer and his backing orchestra who played in a huge hall surrounded by the portraits of our host's disapproving ancestors.

We were here for a party, although until a couple of days ago I'd never even heard of the man who was holding the celebration.

'But who is he?' I asked Derek, one of my current lovers and the guy who'd asked me to accompany him.

To everyone else, Derek was very quiet, very serious – it was only with me that he let his hair down. Not as tall as me, Derek always looked older than his forty-two years. He'd probably got that way making his first million, inventing the technological wizardry to go inside half the world's computers.

'He's one of the richest men in the country,' Derek

answered, 'and so he should be – he seems to own most of it.'

'Why haven't I heard of him?'

'With the sort of money he's got, he can ensure he never has any publicity.'

'How did he get to be so rich?' I wanted to know.

'Having a father who was the biggest landowner in the country helped, I suppose.'

'Where do you know him from?'

'I met him a couple of times,' Derek told me. 'One of his companies owns a minority share in my firm. I don't really know him at all.'

'What are his parties like?'

'No idea. Never been to one. I'm surprised that he invited me.'

'What's the party in aid of?'

Derek shook his head, staring again at the gold leafed invitation, made out to him 'and partner' – which was why Derek had asked me to go with him.

And now we were here, still not knowing why the party was being held. There were hundreds of people milling around in the various rooms, drinking and eating and laughing and talking and dancing. And I seemed to recognize most of them from somewhere – they were all celebrities, famous in their own special-ized fields. Amongst them I noticed at least a dozen guys I'd fucked.

As a liveried waiter offered us a choice of various drinks served in crystal glasses, Derek gazed at the assembled throng.

'Some of the most important people in the country are here tonight,' he said.

'Yes,' I agreed, 'and one of them is standing right next to you.'

He casually glanced to his other side, but when he saw no one he recognized he turned back to look at me. He smiled. 'You?'

I nodded, and I also looked around. 'If you see our host, point him out to me.'

'Of course,' said Derek.

I was wearing a white silk evening dress which fitted so close that I wore no underwear because it would have shown or spoiled the smooth line of the garment. It was long sleeved and hung down to my ankles, but was split halfway up my right thigh. At the front its neck reached my throat, yet the back plunged almost to the base of my spine. Apart from my high heeled white shoes, I wore nothing else. No jewellery, very little makeup. My hair had been permed, and it hung down to my shoulders in a cascade of dark brown tangled curls. And the faint outline of my other curls could just be seen where my dress was stretched tight across my pubis.

Derek met someone he knew, and I saw an old friend of mine, Diana; so my escort and I split up and we mingled. Diana was a beautiful black girl, tall and statuesque, and she'd probably blown as many guys at tonight's party as I had. We talked for a while, drinking and eating the spiced and savoury delights which had been gathered from the far corners of the world, as we compared notes on who was fucking who these days. All the time we both scanned the males in the vicinity, searching out potential lovers, then Diana spotted someone she wanted to get to know, and I was left alone.

I wandered around for a time, speaking to a few people, drinking some more, even dancing; but I soon realized that I was bored, I wasn't enjoying myself. Our host had paid a fortune for a lavish party, but money alone wasn't enough to make it come alive. It all seemed so formal and rehearsed, as though everyone was pretending to enjoy themselves. Most of the guests simply weren't used to relaxing, they didn't know how. Their whole lives had been work, work, work, which was why they'd become so successful – but it had also made them dull, dull, dull. It just wasn't my idea of a party.

Perhaps I was still too young to enjoy it all. Just

about everyone there was older than me, even the waiters and the entertainers. The singer was world renowned, but he was more than twice my age and his music seemed almost classical.

I was hot and sticky, and I went out of the main entrance and down the steps into the open. I felt like being alone for a while, and it was a lovely night, so I decided to explore the grounds of the house. The gardens were magnificent, and I wished I could have seen them during the day, when the flowers were fully open to welcome the sunlight. Marble statues of ancient gods guarded the lawns, one of them a superb Poseidon holding a fish from whose mouth spurted a fountain of water. The water fed a huge pool, and in the moonlight I could see enormous goldfish lazily swimming just beneath the surface. It was very peaceful, and even the amplified sounds from the orchestra couldn't disturb the tranquillity.

But as I listened, I heard another sound – but this time it was faster, more my kind of music. I moved towards where I sensed the new music was coming from, the thudding beat of a rock band. Was there a second party going on, one which I might appreciate more? I hoped so.

I walked on till I came to a two-storey annex by the side of the main building. There was a light at an open window, and here seemed to be the source of the other music. The walls were very old, huge blocks of irregular stone, and the heavy wooden door was held together by strips of iron. It was slightly open, so I pushed my way in. There was no doubt that the sound came from here. A flight of stone steps faced me, worn away by countless years of use. I made my way to the top, finding myself in a long low room.

I realized that I'd made a mistake. This wasn't another party. There were just two young guys at a pool table, and they had a stereo system which was turned up very loud. As well as pool, I saw a ping pong table at the other end of the room, and there was a dartboard on one wall. Another wall was lined with video games. I'd found myself in the staff recreation room.

Before I could retreat, I was spotted. The guy on the furthest side of the table stood up after taking a shot, and he caught sight of me. His companion noticed the direction of his gaze and also looked at me. The first one reached towards a console on the wall and turned a dial, and at once the music volume decreased.

'What are you doing here?' he demanded. 'No one invited you. Fuck off!'

I'd been about to leave, but I didn't want them to think they'd driven me away. So instead I walked closer, my eyes fixed on the two youths – and as I did, I realized they looked exactly the same. They were about eighteen, slender, with short black hair. They must have been identical twins, I realized. They were both clad in jeans and T-shirts, although the one who'd spoken wore a red top, the other green.

'That's not a very nice thing to say,' I said.

'Okay, please fuck off,' the first one told me.

There was a chair by the wall, and I sat down. 'Mind if I watch the game?' I asked.

'You here for the party?' asked the second one, chalking the tip of his cue and then blowing the blue dust away.

'Yes,' I answered. 'But I got bored. This looks more interesting.' I looked him up and down, making sure he was aware of it.

'There's no party here,' the first one told me. 'So why don't you –'

'– fuck off?' I said, glancing at him and smiling slightly. 'Lend me your cue, and maybe I will.'

He bit his lower lip, trying to suppress a smile of his own.

'Never mind Nick,' said the second one, gesturing towards his brother. 'He's in a bad mood 'cos he's just split with his girlfriend.'

'Fucking right,' said Nick. 'The little cunt wouldn't

suck me off, so I got rid of her.' He watched me closely to observe my reaction.

'If your cock's as dirty as your language,' I told him, 'I'm not surprised.'

His brother laughed out loud, slapping his thigh with the palm of his hand.

Nick glanced at the pool table. 'You play, do you?' he asked me. 'You any good with balls?'

'Why don't you let me watch you play with yours?' I suggested. 'Or are you all talk?'

'Give the lady a drink, Simon,' said Nick. 'She'll need it so she can swallow her words.'

So saying, he proceeded to clean up the table, sinking every ball. I didn't know what the rules were, but I could tell he was good.

Without asking what I wanted, Simon handed me a can of beer. That definitely wouldn't have been my choice, but this was some kind of test. I ripped back the ring, and thick brown foam bubbled out. I put my lips to the can, licking up every drop, then tilted my head back and took a swig of beer. Simon and Nick had both been watching me intently, and I wiped my mouth with the back of my hand.

'How come you're not at the party?' Simon asked.

'I got bored with all those old farts,' I told them. I wondered if that might have been the wrong thing to say; I was older than the twins and they might have regarded me with equal disdain. But I wasn't too much older.

Instead Simon nodded, while Nick said: 'I know exactly what you fucking mean.' He started retrieving the balls. 'We're having our own private party, as you may have noticed. You're very welcome.'

'Thanks,' I said, and I stood up and moved by his side. 'How do you play this game? This fucking game, I mean.'

The twins laughed, Nick dropping his cue, and I realized that they must have had as much to drink as me. They were very good looking young men, and I couldn't help wondering whether their pricks were also identical . . .

They each opened another can of beer, and they showed me how to play pool – or pretended to. They were mainly interested in putting their arms around my waist on the pretext of demonstrating the proper cue action, or holding my thighs as they corrected my stance, or seeming to accidentally brush against my boobs as they made sure I held the cue properly. And I enjoyed every moment, feeling their warm strong hands through the thin fabric of my dress. My cunt lips became wet, and I squeezed the muscles of my vagina and imagined that they held a stiff cock between them, wondering whether it would be Nick's or Simon's. It was inevitable that one of them would fuck me. I wasn't going to let the opportunity slip by. My profession allowed older men to screw me, but for relaxation I preferred a young stud thrusting into my twat.

Simon or Nick? Why not both of them? But one of them would have to be first, so which would it be? If they were identical, it shouldn't really matter.

My nipples pressed hard against my dress, their profiles clearly outlined. It was very hot in the room, there was only one window for ventilation. My body was damp with sweat, my dress sticking to my skin, the material becoming transparent where my skin was the wettest – my boobs and thighs, my arms and stomach.

'Hey!' I cheered as I managed to pot my first ball into the top corner pocket.

'That was good,' said Nick. 'The only trouble is, that's the black ball.'

'What's wrong with that?' I asked.

'You're meant to go for the black last,' Simon explained. 'If you pot it too soon, you lose the game.'

I shrugged and leaned the cue against the side of the table. 'I've had enough of this,' I said. 'I'm getting too hot and sweaty . . . and this isn't as much fun as the way I prefer to get hot and sweaty.'

The twins glanced at each other, unsure if I meant what they thought I meant.

Simon turned his head to his brother, whispering in his ear. Nick slowly nodded in agreement.

'Why don't we try a different sort of pool?' he said. 'How about a swim?'

'In that goldfish pond out there?' I asked.

'Can if you want,' said Simon. 'But there's a proper swimming pool at the back of the main house.'

They both looked at me expectantly.

'I haven't got a bathing costume,' I told them, looking serious. I ran my fingers over my breasts then down my hips. 'But I suppose I could swim in this thing.' I nodded. 'Okay, let's go.'

The pool was as amazing as the house. It was huge, an indoor replica of a jungle lake. Its sides were composed of natural rock, and there wasn't a straight line anywhere. There were trees and shrubs and exotic plants growing all around, and there was a huge cage full of brightly coloured tropical birds which screeched and sang. At the far end there was even a waterfall, a sparkling river of water pouring from the higher rocks down into the pool a dozen feet below. It was hotter in there than it had been in the recreation room.

I'd have expected that there would have been other people there, party guests, but the pool was empty. Had I known about it earlier, then this was where I'd have headed.

'Is it all right to be here?' I asked.

Nick shrugged. 'Why not?'

'No one's using it,' Simon pointed out.

We stood by the water's edge, and I kicked my shoes off, dipping my right foot into the water. It felt nearly as hot as a bath.

'It's like a sauna in here,' I said.

'There is a sauna and a cold pool,' Nick told me. 'We can go there instead if you want.'

I shook my head. 'This is fine.'

We'd come through past the changing rooms, but I had no need of them. I pulled at one sleeve of my dress, then the other, tugging the garment down my shoulders and off my arms, then slipping it to my waist. Nick and Simon stared at my bare breasts. I wriggled out of my dress, giving them even more to stare at.

Then I turned and dived into the crystal clear water, kicking back to the top, rolling over on my back and floating on the surface, my breasts and cunt hairs in plain view.

'Come on, boys!' I called, my voice echoing. 'Get them off. Don't be shy. You haven't got anything I've never seen before!'

They looked at each other, and in a moment they were both shedding their clothes, racing to be the first one in the pool with me. They were so fast that I barely caught a glimpse of their cocks – but the main thing was that they both had an erection. The water erupted with two simultaneous splashes as they both dived in. They broke the surface together, thrashing through the water as they raced to where I was.

But by the time they reached where I'd been, I had taken a gulp of air and vanished beneath the surface, forcing myself down so that I could watch them as they approached me – two slim submarines, their torpedoes already primed and aimed. There's something about a hard cock which sets my whole body quivering; but the sight of two was even more magnificent.

With Simon and Nick I had two for the price of one, and now that they were naked I couldn't tell which of them was which. But that didn't matter. They had the necessary qualifications, and that was all I was concerned about.

When they didn't find me, they also dived, but I kicked my legs and swam off, making them pursue me beneath the surface – a strange alien world, where everything happened more slowly, more gracefully.

I had to come up for air, and they were right with me, one on either side. I trod water, flicking my hair out of my eyes, and we were all smiling. Their expressions froze as my hands took a firm grip on each of their cocks, giving them both two or three slow strokes, then their smiles became broad grins. Releasing them, I pushed away and swam rapidly off again, towards the waterfall, turning onto my back and letting gallons of warm water splash down onto my body.

The twins caught up with me, and now it was their turn to touch me. Their hands explored my breasts then moved down to my thighs, two hands reaching my cunt at the same time. I leaned back against the side of the pool behind the waterfall, one hand holding a rocky outcrop to keep myself upright. And I opened my legs, my other hand stretching out and taking hold of the first cock I encountered, pulling it towards my waiting twat.

I didn't know which one of them it was, but the guy whose tool I held moved up in front of me, and his stiff shaft glided easily into me. I groaned with pleasure, letting go of the rock and sinking down onto the vertical shaft of flesh which impaled me. The guy's arms went around my waist, supporting me, and we floated free. He trod water to keep our heads above the surface, and we drifted away from the side, beneath the heavy spray from the waterfall, and towards the centre of the pool.

His cock was deep in my cunt, but his hips could only thrust a little, sliding it an inch or so in and out at a time. And we kept sinking beneath the surface, water pouring into my mouth which was open in sheer bliss. The more he tried to fuck me, the worse it became, and his prick kept slipping out.

The other twin was swimming with us, his hands caressing my body, his head bobbing beneath the surface as he watched his brother trying to fuck me. In the end, as the first one failed again, the second brother pushed him aside and took his place, dragging me below the surface and plunging his cock into my eager cunt. We rolled over and over together in the water, and I could tell that some of the positions which could be tried would be sensational. The only trouble was that we had to keep surfacing for air.

But I kept on experimenting. As one dick was torn from me by the water, I seized the other and carried on fucking as best I could. Finally we found the best way. If I floated supine with one of the twins on his back beneath me and keeping me buoyed up, the other one could lie almost on top of me, above the water, and fuck away for several seconds before either losing his balance or his brother deciding that it was his turn.

I was surprised at the staying power of Nick and Simon. Most guys of their age and virility would have come by then. Instead it was me who had climaxed, and not just once. The warm water flooding in and out of my cunt was like a tide of semen, triggering off my orgasms.

But at last one of them did come. He'd just been driving into me, but then we'd both slipped and sunk below the surface, still joined. I could tell he was desperately trying to keep his prick embedded in me, but as we both thrust out our arms and legs it was inevitable that we would drift apart. And a moment later he climaxed. His cock twitched and spurted, his ejaculation seeming in slow motion because of the water which caught it. His come became streaks of whiteness in the pool, and I tried to cup it in my hands but most of it eluded me. I rubbed what I could trap against my nipples, and then I had to surface again for air.

The guy who'd come spluttered up after me, and he grinned.

'Nick?' I asked.

He shook his head.

'Simon,' I nodded.

'Right second time,' he told me.

I glanced around for Nick, who was floating on his back, his hard cock now a snorkel. If his girlfriend refused to suck him off, then I ought to show him what he was missing – and how if he treated her better, she'd be more inclined to take his prick in her mouth.

Fellatio in a swimming pool is much easier than fucking, I discovered. Nick simply had to stay on his back, I could keep hold of his cock with one hand and stay on the surface with the other. Meanwhile, my lips could suck his wet dick, my tongue sliding up and down its length. And as an extra bonus for me, I had Simon.

He tried to lick my twat, but as it was below the surface all the time he must have kept getting mouthfuls of water. After a few attempts he gave up, and I had to make do with two fingers inside my cunt instead. But it was better than nothing. A lot better than nothing.

Nick was lying back, doing nothing except totally enjoying himself. He had a smug expression on his face, and I was half inclined to almost take him to the brink and then leave him to jerk himself off; but I was enjoying Simon's enthusiastic fingers sliding in me, his knuckles stroking my clit, and Nick's cock felt so good in my mouth – and I hadn't tasted spunk for over a week . . .

My lips engulfed the firm penis, my fist clenched around the shaft sliding the loose skin up and down, and I sensed the first tremor which signalled his climax. I closed my eyes, and when Nick erupted into me I held every drop of his delicious spunk in my mouth, rolling it on my tongue, letting it flow between my teeth, extracting every atom of flavour from the thick liquid before finally swallowing it down.

Simon's fingers slipped out of my cunt, and Nick floated away. I drifted luxuriously on the surface, the gentle flow of water slowly pushing me to the end of the pool away from the waterfall, and I lightly bumped into the rocks. At last I opened my eyes, and the brothers were standing above me. Naked, with identical erections.

I raised my arms, and they pulled me from the water. I sat on the edge of the pool for a few seconds, my feet trailing in the water. Then I stretched out on the ground, and one of the twins knelt by my side.

'Simon?' I said.

He grinned. 'That's right.'

I opened my mouth and also my legs. Simon's hard cock slid between my lips, while Nick's equally firm prick thrust into my cunt, and they fucked me towards infinite ecstasy once again.

Derek hardly seemed to have missed me. My hair was still damp, but he didn't notice.

'Good party,' he commented.

I nodded in agreement, reaching for a glass from the nearest waiter. After all my activity, I needed a drink, but I held the glass in my hand for a couple of minutes without touching it because I didn't want to lose the last delicious taste of semen in my mouth.

I had just finished my drink when I noticed Simon, or maybe it was Nick. Whichever twin it was, he had exchanged his T-shirt and jeans for a white shirt with a black bow tie, black velvet waistcoat, and dark pants with a razor sharp crease. A minute later I saw his brother, similarly clad. For a few seconds I thought they were back on duty, serving drinks. Then I realized that they were talking with some of the guests as though they knew them. I couldn't work out what was going on.

Then someone else attracted my attention, a man who had just entered the room. There wasn't much to distinguish him. He was in his mid-forties, his hair thick but greying, yet somehow my eyes were attracted to him. He moved confidently through the throng, nodding to people who greeted him. He paused when he saw one of the twins, then the other, and the two brothers walked over to him. The man said something and they both nodded, and he smiled easily at them before resuming his stroll through the crowd. Nick and Simon returned to the people they'd been talking with.

I saw that Derek was watching the newcomer, too.

'Who were those two young men that guy was talking with?' I asked him.

Derek frowned a moment. 'Oh, they must have been his sons. He has identical twins.'

The man was staring directly at me now, and although I could already guess the answer I asked: 'Who is he?'

Derek could tell that the guy was heading towards us, and he licked nervously at his lips, wiping his hand against his pants in anticipation of a handshake. 'Our host,' he whispered from the side of his mouth.

'Hello, how are you?' said the man, offering Derek his hand, but his eyes staring at me.

It was as if he could see right into my mind, knew everything about me, my whole life history. Suddenly I felt like a little girl, weak and defenceless. I heard him ask Derek if he'd introduce us, or whether Derek planned to keep me all to himself, but the words hardly registered.

'Your glass is empty,' he said to me. 'Would you like another?'

As if in a dream, he took my glass from my hand. Instantly there was a waiter at his side with a refill.

'Thanks,' I said, accepting the drink from our host. His hand held mine for a moment, and involuntarily my cunt muscles flexed. My labia had been stuck together with Nick's spunk, but now as they opened I felt the warm stickiness of his seed trickle down the inside of my thighs. I smiled at the man.

The man smiled too.

One of the richest men in the country . . . and Simon and Nick were his sons. I wondered if the old saying could be reversed – like sons, like father.

I didn't doubt for one instant that it wouldn't be too long before I found out.

I had just met my future – or as much of the future that mattered.

All Futura Books are available at your bookshop or newsagent, or can be ordered from the following address: Futura Books, Cash Sales Department, P.O. Box 11, Falmouth, Cornwall TR10 9EN.

Please send cheque or postal order (no currency), and allow 60p for postage and packing for the first book plus 25p for the second book and 15p for each additional book ordered up to a maximum charge of £1.90 in U.K.

B.F.P.O. customers please allow 60p for the first book, 25p for the second book plus 15p per copy for the next 7 books, thereafter 9p per book.

Overseas customers, including Eire, please allow £1.25 for postage and packing for the first book, 75p for the second book and 28p for each subsequent title ordered.